Stephen Morris

Memoir, A Novel by Stella Kelly

Austin Macauley Publishers™
LONDON • CAMBRIDGE • NEW YORK • SHARJAH

A CIP catalogue record for this title is available from the British Library.

ISBN 9781528936071 (Paperback)
ISBN 9781528936088 (Hardback)
ISBN 9781528968546 (ePub e-book)

www.austinmacauley.com

First Published (2019)
Austin Macauley Publishers Ltd
25 Canada Square
Canary Wharf
London
E14 5LQ

Chapter One
Memoir

I knew he could not be my father when he mocked me for being a vegetarian at the age of seven and confirmed me as one for the rest of my life. Until his death and beyond, he refused to accept he could not be my father. That is why I never believed anything he told me. Adoption or differences have themed my life of writing. Now that I approach with trepidation the idea of writing outside the academic sphere, I pause on the word, memoir. It should be brief. Not an aide-memoir or a memorial. A stab, I think, at a personal review.

Already, hesitantly, I feel an inner editor jousting with my super ego (for want of a better construct) to get on top of all this. Why not just write a novel? So, in as far as this is my own account of my life, it remains highly imagined. I don't want to write a novel. I do want to get over my academic style. That might take a while.

Walking this morning before I began the memoir, I passed two elderly people. The first touch of autumn—it was a little fresh and the early morning sun glinted with warmth through the still thick canopy of nearly turning chestnut leaves around the square. The elderly couple were clutching hold of each other. It was not the desperation of love but its consequence. Dependence—hard to decipher in their concentrated look of walking together. I could not distinguish who was dependent on who. Or perhaps the dependence was mutual, and their mental and physical afflictions neatly balanced across their lives. That has not been my experience.

The couple, that dependence, I have denied myself in terms of partners and children. Not that I have been without adult companions, a husband and a friend. Or children, Noah, the adopted and largely estranged boy I began to raise. It has been a choice. Yes, I think that is correct, a choice not a consequence of the sequestered life of the thinker and writer I imagined myself to be, to have been.

Estranged and divorced does not mean a complete cutting off from these dear loved creatures who were at one time an occupation and now a fond—if troubled—source of memories. That is so much the case that only a few weeks ago, I sat down with Noah, my adopted son, and Neil his adopted father and my divorced husband. They wanted to have lunch, although the meeting was at my request. My terrible loss of appetite meant I should have preferred coffee, but I gave way to their preference. Momentarily and unusually, I was anxious they would not wish to see me unless it was on their terms. So much has recently changed in how I see the world.

The restaurant in London was modern, slick and stylish. The menu—the usual combination of the novel and the possibly inedible. I simply chose the dishes I thought would be the smallest and least flavourful. Whatever happened to the salad? When the chargrilled baby gem lettuce appeared, my instinct was to ask how it had been washed. When I told Neil, he grimaced and half smiled. He agreed and at the same time, didn't wish to puncture the atmosphere of stylish dining that attracted Noah and helped him to feel secure with his divorced parents and useless adopted mother.

I had wanted to meet to let them know that I was on my way back to Berlin. I shall be there soon and intended to complete this memoir during a prolonged stay there across the difficult winter months. The wind was taken out of my sails completely. Neil announced he was having treatment for an as yet undiagnosed but apparently neurological condition. He told me this in a sanguine way and appeared to find the personal drama one way of coping with what must be a terrifying situation. Clearly, Noah knew, and the matter had been discussed. Noah was simply being very adult in the way that when you are a still young, the terrors of age and disease are as remote as war and lawlessness.

I questioned Neil. I believed him when he told me there was little more to say as he was still at the stage of tests. He believed he was receiving excellent treatment and had been referred to a specialist London hospital. This much we all took in our stride as my attention was removed from the cleanliness or otherwise of the baby gem lettuce. I now cannot remember what else I ate at the lunch. Probably very little of what had been served.

Neil dropped his fork as he helped himself to some potatoes. It fell on the linen tablecloth in front of him. Noah swiftly picked it up and handed it to his dad. I looked until Neil acknowledged my unspoken question that this was a symptom. Noah explained on his behalf that his dad now often dropped things, missed his step and occasionally stopped in mid-sentence having forgotten what he intended to say next. Noah spoke like one of my students at the start of a viva trying to control the questions that would test the extent of their knowledge. Neil added he was beginning to have some difficulty reading. His concentration failed, and the words blurred. His driving licence was suspended.

I wondered and still do. If I hadn't met them for lunch to tell them I was off to Berlin for the autumn and winter whether I would ever have found out about Neil's illness. They both seemed very ready to speak about Neil's condition. That is what they both called it, I forgot. A condition, like the state of maintenance of a building or of a country. They spoke about it, if I recall correctly, to the exclusion of all else. It overwhelmed all other topics of conversation. There was no need for me to speak unless to offer nods of sympathy and a genuine—if shallow—sympathy. No one asked me anything. I mentioned I was off to Berlin. They simply accepted the information. It was nothing surprising. I have lived there on and off for more than twenty years and have an honorary academic post.

I asked Noah about his work, his training now that he had finished his degree. As ever, I am slightly hazy about what exactly he does—to do with the law, at least I am sure he did a law degree. He said he might take some time out to care for his dad. His firm was very sympathetic. Of course we were all very sympathetic, are sympathetic.

So let me get it off my chest. What about me? I can feel Noah's disapproving six-year-old stare as he silently chastised my need for attention. I am sure I left to get away from that silent critical treatment. Heavens, no wonder he is a lawyer.

The reason I am going to Berlin is that I am not well. My symptoms may not be as dramatic as Neil's. I have lost my appetite. I have lost weight and now have almost to force-feed myself to maintain a reasonable appearance. My clothes nonetheless hang off me. My confidence is shattered—not good for an academic—and I am experiencing increasing and irrational feelings of anxiety. I feel a numbness in my fingers and in my toes and have spasms of intense pain across my feet and legs. Sciatica, the GP suggested. She suggested some form of allergy or something to do with my age. She seemed mightily unconcerned. Watch and wait, she said, or she could refer me privately, but there was nothing to warrant any further treatment on the NHS. Sometimes, you just have to adapt as you grow older, we all do, she heart warmingly admonished in the expectation I would vacate her consultation room.

Yet I feel I am dying. Not with the all the rational diagnostics attendant on Neil's symptoms. Just that I am curling up, packing up, clearing off. So that is why I am off to Berlin, and that is why I am having a go at this memoir, and for now, abandoning my latest academic work, *Providence, Not Progress*. Having consulted with a doctor, I consulted with friends. They were more or less sympathetic according to their own take on the situation. One sent me flowers. Another told me there was a lot more hope with cancer these days. Is that the only thing the middle-aged die of, unless it is at their own hand? Others clearly thought me deranged or self-obsessed. No one had any thought as to what I could do about it. My London friends, as I shall call them, proved largely useless. This is another reason for decamping to Berlin. More academic, more artistic, more left wing. I hope for better things.

Andrea, visiting from Germany where she continued to lecture—I have long since given up the podium to younger, brighter women—was indeed helpful. In her view, it was simply the continued conspiracy of my marriage. I had been lured to lunch—although it had been my idea to meet—in the false expectation that Neil and Noah would in any way be interested in my health and my debilitating symptoms only to be completely upstaged. Yet what was more definite about Neil's neurological condition than mine, except he qualified for referral to a top London hospital for tests. We were both suffering physical and psychological ailments. Why weren't his simply dismissed with the indifference that doctors reserve for allergies and age?

Andrea, perhaps with too much zeal in my fragile state of mind, demonstrated that I had been re-imprisoned in my historically conditioned role of wife and mother to listen, tend and heal. Happily, it is a prison I broke free from a long time ago and without regret especially having given the ungrateful Noah something to feel genuinely aggrieved about.

Andrea is correct. I look forward to catching up with her in Berlin. Perhaps she will permit me to attend some of her lectures. I have dutifully read all her books. It was a human thing on my part at least to reach out to Neil and Noah as family. I am sad for Neil, not least because if I lose him (he has already lost me), then two of the men in my life will have disappeared from the continuing present.

So I should speak about Stefan, Stefan Selbst. It is my intention to write chronologically. A memoir with dates. Episodic, yes, but in the right order by the clock and the unashamed intention of bringing forward my theories, concepts and ideas to the general reader in the language of the everyday and with a flavour of myself. Even as I set out on this description of what has mattered, who has mattered to me during the events of my life so far, I am excited by the possibility that my ideas may reach a wider audience than a narrow circle of academics. I believe we write an academic literature today that is less impenetrable than say twenty or thirty years ago. Still it remains pretty dull and boring. Also, the relief, I do not need to reference the literature. You will have to take it on trust that what I say rests on a firm foundation of a lifetime's study, teaching and reading. This is already a pleasurable release from the academic grove. A coming out, I believe.

Unlike Neil, Stefan was a great artist. His death was for me a terrible blow. It was a physical jolt into numbness and then a succeeding emptiness. I was there, in Berlin, right through those dreadful end days. The lung cancer was aptly inevitable given his filthy and self-imposed regimen of smoking. One reason, not the foremost, why we were always friends not lovers. The smell of tobacco revolts me as much as the thought of eating meat. His lunatic ideas and more lunatic art formed me again after my failure to live up to Neil and Noah's ideal woman, wife, mother construct. So much of the art is destroyed, either through its own wild performative feats or because of its inherent fragility of material or media. Like theatre, I feel those of us left behind have only the memory of the event and sometimes the unacted script. The impact of these remnants reminds and reinforces memory as memorial. Thinking of him, remembering his work, thrills me.

He was and is big in the art world—internationally and in Germany and Berlin especially. Another reason for going to Berlin to die is that I can visit some of his greatest preserved works in the beautiful post-industrial, post war, post wall debauched buildings where they hold their ground as a magnificent testament to his understanding of human need and greatness. The rubble of history and of our minds—that is how he spoke to me of his working when he took me on. That will need some careful re-examination when I come to describe it in greater detail later. How I ended up being so closely connected to him and to his work? How it inspired my own direction of thought? How his death and my need to find my way in an absence of ideas has led to the temporarily—permanently when I die—abandoned work *Providence, Not Progress*?

Death and dying is so nationalistic. The British white elite hide the dying and make pomp of the death. I remember seeking to reconcile this when I lived next door to Massachusetts General Hospital where the dying took ages, and then the dead were simply corpses left in body bags at an outside door each afternoon to be collected for disposal. If Stefan is exemplative, the German way is mechanical and focused on a series of predictable and carefully engineered stages. This is no way heartless. It is not an absence of kindness. It didn't work for my cultural coordinates which desired and required a much more close intertwined emotional and caring process. Caring with love, is that too trite. I could not get close enough to him and maybe simply blamed the system. This is not a disciplined and thought through account. It is still too soon—too soon but much of a decade—and I am using a language of nationality to hide behind in protecting my own too rawly experienced feelings.

Stefan's ego was so large, it was impossible to relate to him without implicitly giving way to worship of a distractingly personality cult type. Released from the imprisonment of my London life as wife and mother, this was an astonishing pull. It fed the overlooked part of myself that was the highly successful academic and think tank wonk (and breadwinner) in the previous life. Stefan attracted people. He was not attracted to people. He sifted the people attracted to him according to his need and their quality. Nobody got ousted if they were willing to be put to work on project Stefan. It suited me. It suited Andrea who led Project Stefan's feminista wing. It was all hopelessly contradictory in a way that revealed the power politics of society the same way 60s and 70s architecture undid the facades of control.

Stefan died in 2010 at the age of 53, and after living there for five years, I left Berlin and returned to London. Andrea said it was ok when I told her I was going to be in London during the funeral. She grieved more obviously than I did. I mean she was more emotional. She told me she wept at the memorial and gave a beautiful tribute lecture as part of the goodbye conference she organised for Stefan. She robustly defended his masculinity in the way only great feminists can. I did nothing. I lived through her emotions. I couldn't speak at the conference and was and am deeply grateful to Andrea that she forgave me straight up unasked. I was absent, so maybe she thought I might as well be absent properly. The job, as I knew but didn't acknowledge to myself, was a political set up for a poorly conceived public policy invented to appear to be doing something about something and didn't survive the 2015 election.

Instead of a memoir, I should be collating a book of what I remember Stefan saying to me. Intimately speaking, if the bonding of intellects could have some physical expression. Let me start with this. "You are more interesting than your books— but people are more interesting than knowledge."

So since 2015, I have been living back in Berlin, the city to which I fled in 2005. Andrea has a daughter, now an adult, of course. She raised her with her long-term partner, but since her daughter has left home, they have separated. I wonder if I am some sort of substitute for one or other or both of these women. The flat is gorgeous. I occupy the daughter's room. I've asked her. She doesn't object. She is glad, she says, that mum has the company.

I watch Andrea each morning as we always breakfast together. She is, like me, older now. Unlike me, she still works. Her breakfast is light; an egg, boiled, or some fruit. She makes coffee, and I thank her for the large mug she brings me with microwaved milk. I watch her eat slowly and delicately. There is a big respect for my vegetarianism—a separate shelf in the fridge and the freezer. Careful cleaning of pots and implements. Andrea prides herself on her hospitality, and I am truly grateful as this makes for a companionship that I have not known for a long time. Perhaps have never known.

Breakfast is over. I tidy up. I place the used items in the dishwasher. Use a damp cloth to wipe up crumbs and spills. Put away unused plates. Andrea disappears. I know she is putting on her make up in her room. She wears only a little, a small indulgence in her appearance that I have always found gorgeous, complete, lovely. She re-appears and checks the weather on her phone and then double checks by looking outside. It is difficult to gauge temperature from our (her) third floor flat. We prepare to part for the day. She puts on her coat or whatever is appropriate for the weather and the season, picks up her backpack with her computer and books and we gently kiss each other on both cheeks to wish one another a good and successful day. The door closes, and I am left to myself.

Andrea, I know, will take the U Bahn to the university where she will either work in the library or teach. Her courses remain very popular, and she works very hard to keep them up to date. She shows me some of her lecture materials, and I have indeed attended one of her courses. They slightly terrify me with their confident use of media that is new to me, but she explains, essential to keep the interest of the students who take this for granted.

We keep in touch on the phone. Messages at various points in the day. Our plans, together or apart, for the evening. I suppose in many ways, the lives of a married couple. I get to know her friends. I like them, and they like me, I think. After all we tend to be academics or from the arts. Some of them remember me from when I was here before with Stefan. We tend not to speak of Stefan so much. He raises strong opinions and accompanying emotions. Andrea knows I admire him. She says little. I think she thought he was a misogynistic git. That is true. We should really discuss this, but you reach a stage when it is unnecessary and unhelpful. It doesn't need to intrude on our domestic arrangements. Sometimes I wonder how long this will continue. I wonder if Andrea thinks about this too.

When this started, when I returned to Berlin, I was resistant to accepting Andrea's invitation. I stayed for a while in a tourist hotel in Kurfurstendam, away from the areas where I had stayed previously in Ostkreuz and Schonhauser Allee. She prevailed in part, because my sense of dying was so overwhelming, I became frightened. She has always accepted that I am dying. Her implicit care for me is the foundation of our lives in her flat together. She is the companion of a dying woman, a woman only a little older than herself but retired, no longer active, withdrawing from the world and deeply anxious. An anxiety that sometimes prevents me from taking the U Bahn as I become so frightened on the platform—frightened that I will fall off—that I can barely walk along its length or board a train.

In the mornings, in fact right now, after Andrea has left for her work, I sit at the kitchen table that I have cleared from the breakfast things. I open my computer and start to write. That is where this memoir is being written. This is background. Just imagine me writing each day, a little at a time, in the kitchen of my dear friend Andrea's flat just on the old East Berlin side of the wall close to Rosa Luxembourg Platz. Even the names give me a shiver of history. All that I love is right here, and for the first time, I savour it, and I am dying.

At the lunch with Neil and Noah, it was not possible to tell them any of this. Despite myself, I felt too much love for Neil. He spoke so flatly of his illness that he could not disguise his fear. Noah was the same. I think of them there, sat politely at the stylish restaurant—to impress me, themselves? Who cared about the food? Neil pushed it around his plate. His appetite was clearly gone. Was that another of his symptoms?

Neil asked me about myself. There was every opportunity to tell him about my health and my plans to debunk to Berlin. Yet, I could not do it. His illness took precedence. Noah would only think it was one upmanship on my part. I couldn't afford, I knew, further to strengthen his already strong resentment. If I did not act the loving ex-spouse, Noah would never see me again. That would make me sad. Not because I particularly wanted to see Noah, even occasionally, but because it was, even after all I had done, unfair for him to decide never to see me again. So, as Andrea gently says—usually in the evening as breakfast is a simpler and kinder time—I simply allowed the past to re-enact itself and for me to be recast in the role I had jettisoned successfully. Successfully that is unless I find myself with these two men, Neil and Noah, who added up to a part of my early life—more later—and accompanied the successes, triumphs really, that heralded the all too bright start of a career.

That slanting light as the autumn was in full flower and the sun lower in the sky when I left the restaurant and crossed the square, admiring again the trees—their age, dignity and beauty. Across the square and down the side street towards the tube—one of the old-fashioned stations with a lift and ceramic tiles in the colour of the line on the underground map. We had parted well. Neil had promised to let me know as soon as he heard anything more definitive. I was balanced, matching his sanguinity and Noah's frightened impassivity. I contained them by containing me, forgetting me. We agreed to meet around Christmas, but I knew I would be gone, and for both of them, Berlin represented my betrayal. They would never come there, and I would not even be an afterthought for them when I was there, banished from their minds.

The familiar street was strangely different as I came at it from the square. It was not on account of the light of the beautiful day as I knew this place well. That is why Neil chose the restaurant. So obvious, because this was where we had spent so much time, but that was precisely the reason. The street changed, because the old university halls of residence where I had spent a year as an undergraduate was demolished and replaced by a much larger building. I looked at the reception area. Still apparently for students but no longer the institutionalised semi dormitory type arrangement I had been used to. Now a gradpad for discerning students to socialise and exercise, store their bikes and visit the bar and fast food outlet. The place, or its former version, I now remembered, where Neil and I first had sex, had quite a lot of sex as I remember. Which made me laugh right there and then. He is a romantic fool. Dying and he wanted to revisit his sexual exploits of youth.

I laughed, aghast that I had simply forgotten. I was aghast equally that the place where I had romped with sexual pleasure was now demolished, made way for the next crew to romp in their own way.

The past can be a sentimental territory. Neil's sentimentality, unintelligible to Noah who was too raw, governed the whole relationship extended now to this lunch. I silently breathed in the sentiment. I allowed it to fill my emotional space. I allowed it, as part of someone else's story, but a story in which I appeared, to make me very sad. Right there I was clobbered by sadness washing over me like a tidal wave. Then the secondary quake happened, the sense of jilting repugnance at having been ambushed in this cheap way, but the cheap obviousness of Neil's ploy. He contradicts the intellect. He tried, as he always did, to make the superficial emotion win out. I yearned for the lamentation Neil and Noah both denied for the real sadness of Neil's condition.

Would I have enjoyed my life more if I weren't a vegetarian is a question similar to how I would have got on if I had lived the traditional professional existence my parents desired. It is as wrong to claim that my academic life was in defiance of them as to say I believe I deserved different parents. I do not winge on that front. My parents are the ones I got. What may be truer is that they gave me a taste for defining myself by contradicting the expectations laid out for me in terms of gender, family and class. I am equally open to the argument that my quest for some autonomy, some sense of personal identification and achievement apart from my background is itself the defining demographic feature of my generation. It was what I find most dispiriting about Noah. He was truly an outsider. Maybe that is the difference, not a generation that has retreated from the adventures of its forerunners.

I learnt from my elder brother to elude the distinctively physical approach my dad took to enforcing a discipline of compliance. A compliance he demanded with a visceral righteousness with his views of the world and with the prejudices these projected. It had the same religious fervour and devotion of a different age without the need for the respectability of fake religion. He believed in nothing except himself. It must have taken a supreme level of energy to maintain such a confidence when an increasingly present and rampant media showed him he was wrong. My mother was, I guess, his greatest believer, and perhaps that was enough. I imagine her doubts, supressed with all the devotion of a 19th century nun.

The key lesson my brother taught me was no provocation. Not one he ever learnt himself. Growing more conscious as an infant, the seasons made themselves most clear through the return of winter and the accompanying cold. The heating that we now take so for granted had not arrived in the house where I grew up. Instead, we retreated to the parts of the house where the cold was least able to penetrate. Everywhere was cold, but in the room with the coal fire and in the kitchen where the water boiler burnt gas, there was an attempt to keep it at bay. The smaller you were the colder you were. I think this is a physiological fact, although I didn't know it then.

He must have been ten. Winston, the elder brother and my only other sibling, had visited some friends. They had introduced him to central heating. He described to me in awe a house where every room was of a constant and pleasant warmth. Where taking your clothes off to go to bed was not a trial of the will tantamount to punishment for existence. It sounded heavenly. In fact, let me be clear, it is heavenly if you have experienced its absence. It makes winter quaint and fun. It defines progress—well more on that despicable topic later.

My brother's mistake was to communicate to dad our need to adopt this advance of the human race in our own home. Being ten, his approach was possibly doomed to fail. His comparison of the friend's house cast our own in a negative light. Dad took it as an insult, to himself and to his beliefs. His view was that the friends must be soft, the cold was a friend and enabled us to be resilient and tough. He didn't want a soft son who would grow up to be—I leave a blank for the reader to complete with their own homophobic appellation.

My brave ten-year-old brother fought back. He told Dad that he was wrong (big mistake) and (much worse) it showed he was a fool. He told Dad he was saying that to cover the fact that we couldn't afford it because our family was too poor, not good enough, and while he was at it because dad didn't really love us. Dad didn't approve of love.

Then the all too familiar beating began. These beatings would carry on until Winston became physically strong enough to resist them. That was only a short time before he was old enough to quit the now centrally heated family home. This beating I remember because of its severity, and because it was so public, happening right in front of me, terrifying me.

Dad fetched his slipper, and Winston made a run for it. When Dad caught him, he hit him hard several times with the slipper. Winston wriggled and tried to escape Dad's grasp, and as a result, was hit in the face leaving a sore, red mark. Finally, he did give Dad the slip and made for the stairs. Dad, infuriated that Winston refused even to submit to his punishment chased him and caught him half way up the stairs. Dad abandoned the slipper. It was as if his wrath so consumed him that he needed the violence to be directly at his own hands. He beat him with slaps and punches. He grabbed him by the neck so that he looked like a chicken, his limbs flailing, about to be butchered. Then, pausing his attack, Dad started to pull off his clothes. He humiliated Winston, ripping the shirt and shorts he was wearing, pulling off his pants so that he was naked half way up the stairs. Dad had a plan. He dragged the boy up the stairs towards the bathroom. I heard the water being run into the bath. I knew he would force Winston to take a bracing cold bath—as Dad himself did every morning.

Mum went to make a cup of tea. These events were never spoken of, never discussed, because we all pretended they never happened. A man unable to express how he felt unless it was through violence. I never asked him how he felt. I never offered him an opinion.

Chapter Two
The Politics of Make-Believe

These were the wonderful years. It is 1975. I am 18 years old and sexy. Everything is equally possible and impossible. I cannot keep up with myself. I thrust myself into the set, into the spotlight. I hide away. I observe. I note. I am principled and daredevil, unsure which way to go, wanting to go every way at once. That is the tenor of the times. Still everything is possible. The sixties light the future. I ignore the politics of Britain. The lack lustre, the three-day week, nothing working and an inability to create. I associate it with the fear of my parents' generation, of the overhang of the war. The political world of the seventies is unconnected with the generation growing up in the warm embrace of the sixties. Vietnam just proved the point.

I think I am capturing who I was at that time. It is a Stella I have come back to with the affection of a later parent, the parent I should have preferred to the tight, afraid pair I got. You cannot help but ask what if, even as I chastise my university students for wasting time mourning the parents they truly deserved. My brother and I, if we had parented ourselves—which largely I suspect we did—but as parented as our adult selves, what then?

It was still ten years to the big breakthrough. That came with the publication and reception of my first academic text, *The Politics of Make-Believe*. Like all my work, it challenged the orthodoxy of the progressive social sciences. It depended on creating the illusion that the anti-establishment of the past had been sterilised into a current day orthodoxy of a failed academic creed. History is always made that way. Be ahead of it.

I knew a breakthrough would come. I knew this in 1975 before I had even begun to think what I meant by such a term. Yes, I was eager and impatient, but my timing was good or my luck was. Sooner and it would have been dismissed as adolescent, prodigy material, not to be taken seriously except as the imitation tricks of a cleverly trained pet. Yet at 28, I was just old enough to survive those kind of accusations and be received instead as the herald of a new generation in touch with the future possibilities of my academic discourse. Actually, so many years later, I think that would be a valid interpretation of *The Politics of Make-Believe*. Of course it was that work which connected me—although I only found this out later—with Stefan.

I am not just randomly jotting down thoughts about my younger self. I have decided, may I remind you, to be chronological. A little boring, so I will try to liven it up with the occasional flashback (and flash forward), but in the end it is much easier. I think there is no alternative but to describe events in my life in the order in which they happened. The larger challenge is to describe events that are exceptionally cerebral. I wish to write the autobiography of my intellectual life, with interplays of actual meetings, people and things that happened. This may be a little dull, I fear. That also undermines the purpose of my memoir as a good way in for people to get hold of my thoughts unencumbered with the detritus of academic studies.

In 1975, I didn't bother about these things. I synthesised them in creating a personality that had the volatility of non-stop lava, overflowing last week's now cold and solidified version of myself.

One of the boys around, who liked me more than I liked him—but he was ok—called me fickle. We were staying back at a friend's house after a gigue. There were a few of us, and we had the run of the place as the adults were away. We were making out, and I told him that I would have sex with him, but it was because it would be good to have sex. He called me fickle. The same constant issue that haunts us as adults. Men who see the opposite of possession as rejection. It wears me out. It wore me out then. I know he will have gone off to his university then settled down somewhere. A side of happiness that has never been possible for me. There is a hierarchy of happinesses that corresponds to a hierarchy of ethics, where the greatest happiness is the happiness that attaches to the rights and freedoms of the individual, discrete from the discriminatory classes that society imposes. The lower classes of happiness—love, marriage, children, that kind of thing—are always eclipsed by rights and freedoms. Yet the cost is profound, for the lower classes of happiness are easier to achieve, but once eclipsed are never so sweet again. I don't think that boy's class of happiness will have been eclipsed. If his wife has left or betrayed him and his children grown away, he will be puzzled and hurt not enlightened.

I love to use these words. They are the make-believe that made my reputation as the slayer of orthodoxies built on incomprehensible language, describing apparently concrete but irreplicable concepts.

Much later, I heard Stefan refer to *The Politics of Make-Believe* in a workshop on the destruction of the self. We had known each other for more than a year, saw each other most weeks unless Stefan was away exhibiting. We often had a quick lunch, goodies bought from delis in Berlin which, if warm enough, we would nibble outside where we could find a sunny spot. I asked him after the lecture about the reference to the book I had written 20 years before. He had been given it by a friend and had read it transfixed. It had become the manifesto for his artistic growth, he claimed. I wonder now, as I did then, who was that friend and how on earth my book could have turned up in East Germany four years before the wall came down.

Stefan did speak about East Germany where he grew up and studied in Dresden. It always strikes me as odd that the leader of art as an anti-capital political movement should have spent his first 40 years in East Germany. He never saw it that way. Capitalism was something you experienced differently in different parts of the globe. You opposed it because it itself opposed social justice. You opposed it by the creation of different understandings and possibilities in the world. His was just one of these—art.

Actually the boy, he was called Graham, the boy who called me fickle did hang around for a while. It is wrong simply to exit him from my memoir, because I am embarrassed. It is ridiculous to be embarrassed about Graham. Also, Graham reappears later. I cannot write him out. It would be unfair and unkind. It would make the story untrue.

He was deadly serious. He valued being clever the way a stockbroker values a blue chip stock. Like all of us, he was clever up to a point. His difficulty was that the over emphasis he placed (yes, this is me speaking) on being clever meant he never could see that it didn't add up to anything much in the real world. I was definitely a prize, and he was willing to pay an emotional price to hang on to me. I led him a dog's life and that for me—hence my embarrassment—was part of the fun. We hung out at weekends and in the vac despite being at universities at opposite ends of the country.

Then, when I was in the after glory of the publication of *The Politics of Make-Believe,* he tracked me down. He was now in the early slog of a career as a university lecturer. I never thought of my work that way. His university, the staid, elderly dowager, and mine was the new, bright sixties campus. He tracked me down there. It wouldn't have been hard given the notoriety of what I had written. I asked him why he did that when I rang him after he had written to me saying he would like to catch up. He said it was a bit because he was curious now I was famous. He asked too. Why had I rung him in response to his letter? I don't think he had expected me to do that. I should have said as a penance for letting him hang around me as an undergraduate while I carried on with the other guys—including Neil, of course—and for leaving him high and dry as soon as we both graduated. I was curious. That is what I told him, and that was a greater truth when I think about it now. I was curious how his life was turning out. He was my compare and contrast.

We met in Leamington Spa as I was on my way to Birmingham to give a guest lecture, and he was teaching nearby. He was warm and generous. Typically, he had chosen a trendy vegetarian café that he thought would appeal to me. He was confident. He looked like a kind man in his late twenties. He told me about his academic studies and deferred to my super stellar rise to fame. There was no resentment. He asked me if I was interested in or minded him speaking about his girlfriend—and of course that was exactly what I wanted to know about. She taught PE in a secondary school. They were living together and the life sounded something of an idyll. They were undecided on kids.

I also told him about my life so far, so to speak. Neil was just beginning to lurk as a possibility but was insufficiently in focus as a lover to be distinguished from the two or three others I had taken at that time. I didn't mention them. I simply indicated that

19

my relationships were as they always were—fluid and indefinite. I didn't need to say anymore as he knew this from experience.

What he was really interested in was *The Politics of Make-Believe*. The book, written out of my doctoral thesis, was simple in its underlying idea. That scientific knowledge is less important than prevailing beliefs and that success in politics meant harnessing these to achieve power. It was novel, because it attacked not only the natural sciences but their distant cousins— the social sciences, declaring both to be equally subjective in their use of data and experiment to create the goal of political control. To this day, I do not think the scientific community paid any attention or were troubled or even interested in these ideas. For the humanities, it provided a weapon of attack for the quasi-intellectual middle class media and fuelled the reaction against the permissiveness and intellectual orthodoxies of the sixties and seventies.

Graham listened intently and with interest. He offered some direct criticism. He had read the book and the accompanying media commentary. Weren't the ideas a little jejune? I explained that they were in fact accessible, and that was to solve a problem with most conceptual thinking in social science for over 20 years. He also challenged my own politics. Had I had a sea change from my straightforwardly socialist stance at university?

It was a sensible and good challenge. In my defence, the ideas had attracted me then, and I had followed them to what appeared a satisfactory, if far from profound conclusion. I am omitting from this memoir, as has been my intention from the start, the underlying philosophical and social science references and thinking that were certainly present in the doctorate and in a more watered down version (but with a great bibliography!) in the book. What I understand later is that *Make-Believe* was such a transitory phase for me. I passed through it on my own intellectual growth. It still sells well. The ideas are solid and easy to grasp. At that stage, I was still forming a more coherent understanding, a coherence that would itself be a form of disintegrated knowing and not knowing of how as a self I am. What fun as now I am dying, and no one is willing to believe or confirm it, but I believe/make-believe it.

Not sure how it came up when we were talking about something that had happened to us in London when we were a couple. Crossing the Mall to St James Park, a youngish American tour guide was speaking to a group of equally young American tourists. Quite a large group, so he was needing to speak loudly. He was pointing at Admiralty Arch and telling them that the British Empire was a very sensitive subject in the UK, and Brits avoided speaking about it, because of all the atrocities and terrible things that had taken place. Graham and I were walking directly behind the speaker, and the crowd of tourists were suddenly laughing. I turned to see Graham shaking his head in disagreement, and that was causing the laughter. I started laughing too and also shook my head. By the time the tour guide had caught on and turned to see what was causing the disturbance, we had already walked past.

It was a tiny moment of delight. Graham had raised it as his example of make-believe. Were Brits sensitive speaking about the British Empire? Neither of us thought so at the time of the incident or when we met for that lunch. It had triggered for Graham his own academic explorations, with a resurgence of history as great people, places and events. Nelson and Churchill or Clive and Kitchener. History as statues, war memorials, plaques and the context in which they were erected. Did we really speak about such things when we were undergrads? It is difficult to distinguish what we know now from what we knew then. Equally difficult to know which parts of which knowledge is most worth believing.

As a writer of my own memoir, I try to thread together events in some causal way. The lunch with Graham steadied me just as I could have detonated in the publicity aftermath of *Make-Believe*. The tourists laughed at the justifiable ribbing of the authority of their own guide as if to say how could he possibly know. Graham is one of the different selves I publicly inhabited through those earlier years. The lunch was not a mistake. It was something else, because there is no word for the opposite of mistake. A mistake is a contradiction of what is correct, but it has no direct antonym. Its opposite has to be described, because a not-mistake is everything else. Everything we believe in. The make-believe of the tour guide, his mistake not theirs.

It is Stefan who comes to mind, not Neil, when I relate how Graham and I met that time. Was it Stefan who asked if the history of empire was Nelson and Churchill or Clive and

Kitchener; that all histories of empires are histories of memorial, of statue? It seems unlikely Stefan would know enough, although the sentiment and the mode of expression are all his. Have I taken Graham's words and re-invented them in the style of Stefan? Is that how a memoir works, it re-invents the past in a better, more improved, more coherent way. Just like how and why we tell stories.

I don't remember how the Leamington lunch ended. I imagine we knew it was unlikely that we would see each other much or at all. I expect that was more or less what Graham had wished to achieve. I would not be a great stabiliser in his relationship with the gym teacher he spoke of with such affection. It was a Graham event. A careful and thoughtful gesture to enable a better ending than before, laced with his own evident curiosity and sense of shareholding in my success. It would be something, I imagine, he would carefully curate in his life as mine continued to count public success, academically and in public policy. All that has brought me here.

As you grow older, old, as I now am, do you learn less and remember more? To learn is to encounter for the first time, and to be changed. To remember is to encounter what you once learnt and to remember how you were changed. Or, with a person or a place perhaps to encounter the sensation of how that had been as music recalls a past sense of who you once were. So it was with Graham, then and now. A fondness based in the thought of who and how I was with him. Not a shadow or a photo, but a tune half hummed. So that whatever has happened and although neither of us can ever know it does not diminish or erode a memory.

The make-believe of the title pings now against my sense of my teenage and young adult self. Graham provides a countering viewpoint outside that person I was. I am now the one curious, but not quite curious enough to want to find out, whatever happened to Graham. Remember the Friends Reunited version of the web. That didn't survive the make-believe of our actual lives, and how we believe in them, the magic of the web.

Perhaps Graham is on my mind, because it was on the way to the lecture that opened the next door. I hadn't been paying too much attention to who I was lecturing to. Usually I was just an add-on to a more distinguished and older group of academics at various conferences. I was ok with being the spice and not slow to use my youth and gender to advantage. It is difficult to explain how sex worked then. In the midst of the AIDS epidemic, we were lost in the sentimentality of the sixties sexual revolution. Liberated and frustrated in equal measure. It was never so much fun as at university.

I thought the guy in the suit, in his forties I would have thought, was coming on to me when he came up to me after the lecture. He told me he had found it very interesting. He wanted to know where I intended to take my studies now. His appearance was very different from the academics who usually attended these events. He also appeared to have some understanding of the ideas I presented, but in a way that he openly acknowledged was superficially acquired. I told him a little bit more about how the make-believe work primarily ought to inform the relationship between social sciences as an academic discipline and the creation and implementation of public policy. I could give him any number of examples. Road safety, protecting the countryside, funding healthcare. He listened with more than politeness.

At some point, this stopped being a casual conversation over a coffee in the conference reception and became more like the job interview I later clocked it was intended to be. He gave me his card and explained that his firm had been retained by the government to scope a new public agency. It was all part of shaking up Whitehall, making it more relevant, focused and business like. My book, apparently, had caught the attention of a senior and influential minister. Remember, we are talking the mid-eighties here.

Our next meeting was at his office in London. I loved it. It was a perfectly decorated regency period house in a street of similar buildings in Mayfair. The incredibly attractive and well-dressed receptionist showed you into a waiting area that I imagined straight from Harley Street. Then a dinky secretary appeared ushering you into a room that was more like a library or hotel living room. Soft furnishings, occasional tables, the offer of coffee in expensive white porcelain. I lapped it up. Stefan said I was suborned. That is unfair. I was tantalised by the wealth and by the power that were ostentatiously present.

Colin, his name was Colin, came into the room as if he lived there. I took time to notice that it was not just that he was dressed in a suit—no longer out of place as it had been in Birmingham—but that it was a beautifully cut suit. In this expensive office, looking out over Mayfair, I realised that this was the establishment. I was in it and could be part of it. So I asked him why anyone in this government of all governments would want an anarchist like me to help. As I asked the question, I added the answer. I was exactly the right person to shake up Whitehall. I didn't care if I was being suborned—to answer Stefan back after all this time—I couldn't resist my own thesis that I wanted to believe I could subvert the whole damn thing and anyway have a great time trying.

Governments need ideas. They do not have to be good ideas. As *Make-Believe* pointed out, governments need to have ideas people want to believe in. Ideas that are advantageous to the government's own idiosyncrasies. Even incredible ideas can be made believable. Credibility is a sleight of hand perfected by a population brought up on science. Science knows. That is how we understand and control the future. Science provides answers. That is how it is shown to people. Not real science but the science of comfort that is fed day and night in the scientific age. That government, back then in the eighties, and each since has had to live with science. Success has depended on marrying an unimaginable scientific certainty to belief, so that people believe what they are told is happening. That it is science.

Colin was so confident in knowing I was the right person for the job. He explained the risks and opportunities—his language—and what this would mean for me personally. There was an expectation that I would leave my academic post on a secondment to the firm. I was surprised then, but would not be now, that the arrangements had already been worked out in principle with my university employers. Colin was gently sarcastic when he mentioned the scarcity and desirability of government grants in social science research. My university would benefit well from my absence. The secondment arrangement, he explained, meant I would not need to give up my secure job. He made the offer sound generous and corrupt.

At the firm, I would work as an associate on scoping the project for what was already being called the *Evidence into Action Institute*. With glaring superciliousness, Colin immediately adopted its acronym—EIAI. EIAI was to become my project to influence and support change in public policy and in the working of government departments. I need hardly tell you the salary was generous.

Nothing in my child or early adult experience had prepared me for this. I had not sought such advancement. I had never imagined working in Mayfair, with governments and their agents. If anything, I had imagined overthrowing government, undermining the establishment, working in jeans in some bombed out government office to set up some interim people's administration.

Colin asked me if I would like another coffee. I said nothing. He understood, he said, I was perhaps surprised, taken aback. He would leave me. He hoped I could ring him in the next 24 hours to tell him my decision. Things did not stand still in government. This was a small window.

When I reached the street, I was not quite sure where I was. I had used the A to Z to find the office. Now I didn't want the distraction of fishing it back out of my bag and looking up map references. I couldn't be far from somewhere in London more familiar than these narrow, expensive streets of houses. I walked until I found myself in what I realised, looking at the stark outlines of the US Embassy, was Grosvenor Square. This was a place of protest, of demonstration, against those forces of the military industrial complex that had, so I thought and probably still do, disfigured our natural, beautiful world. Looking at the embassy I knew I would accept because I couldn't resist. The answer to the question I had asked Colin, about how an anarchist could help at the heart of government remained the same despite his conscious refusal to answer it himself. He knew I had answered it for myself. He never had needed to as he answered to certainties not ambiguities.

Immediately, I needed to know how to do this on my terms. I would need to be bought heart and soul if I were to succeed. I knew that then. I would use their means to maintain a grip, a personal stamp, on the project. I would seduce Colin.

The difficulty is remembering accurately, or even at all. When you seek to write something true about your own life, it is necessary to be truthful about the lives of others. Is Colin's infidelity in his affair with me known to those around him? Anyone reading this memoir will readily identify who he is. Of course, I have changed his name but not too much else about him. EIAI became a real, even infamous, government agency responsible for—if I'm frank—some serious blunders and missteps. Yet I cannot write about myself with any hope of doing justice to this memoir without speaking about a man who became my lover and then my, what would one say, guide?

The affair itself was straightforward. Colin's needs were sexual. He was shocked the first time I proposed we sleep together. We were having coffee in the living room or library where we first met in the firm's offices. I just told him that I would like that. His shock was because I don't think anyone had asked him to go to bed with them before. I understood his world as little as he understood mine. His reluctance had to be overcome, so I set out to understand what prevented him from immediately agreeing. I knew he wanted to have me, and with the element of surprise of my initial proposal, he failed to contain his evident desire.

There were, in my analysis, three major obstacles: first, his fear of AIDS, secondly his fear of being found out, and thirdly his preference for not gratifying what he felt were his own more sordid needs. None of this was encouraging to me. I considered upbraiding this pillar of the capitalist world on his failure to live up to a reputation for the ruthless exploitation of resources. I rapidly rejected this. More feral, I used love. I was extremely careful to explain I had no interest in upsetting his marriage or family life. I was, after all, in an increasingly regular and more monogamous relationship with Neil myself. I sold him the fantasy of romance. That I was carried away with an ecstatic passion. That we owed it to ourselves to fulfil this as adults and not miss this opportunity for romance.

It worked a dream.

The autumn in Berlin approaches more rapidly than in London. The leaves are two weeks earlier turning and now most have fallen. Andrea is gone to the university. Breakfast was a feast of companionship. I enjoy more and more these days with her. I am writing now as I do most mornings at Andrea's kitchen table. Bashing out words one by one on a machine that did not yet exist when Colin and I were romantically engaged back then. Now, I still feel that twinge of love for him. An impossible love for a man who was strong, formidable at the firm, at the

26

workplace, in the corridors of power. It is everything I hated, continue to hate. Everything that Andrea, Stefan, everyone I have valued would revolt against and be revolted by. Yet he remains a real place where I established a strange credibility across differences that made human beings appear to belong to different species.

Even in the short time since I arrived here in Berlin, my health has deteriorated further. Most obviously, it is that things take me much longer. A morning is spent writing, and I feel exhausted. In the afternoon, I need to lie down and rest. Making a cup of coffee, as I will do after finishing this chapter, will take me the best part of an hour—and then drinking it and trying to fit in lunch. A positive consequence is that time now comes in larger chunks. As it takes me longer, I think not about hours or parts of hours, but half days or whole days. I won't spend an hour writing, but a morning. I won't visit the Altes Museum for a morning but a day. This is as restful as the gently chilling weather outside. Tasks are more strung out and more enjoyable. There are more pauses—for thoughts and their absence.

The other more upsetting part of my illness is the anxiety. It makes me frightened to catch the U or S-Bahn or to walk too far into the Tiergarten. It is not always there. It reminds me of altitude sickness. For no reason, when its strikes, I am mentally afflicted and physically paralysed. I fear the loss of my possessions. It is a little like going crazy, losing control.

I am trying to understand whether the anxiety is somehow connected to dragging up all this past stuff. The contrast between the self-confident young woman who seduced the cocksure management consultant as an act of will and this anxious, now dying woman could not be greater. It is a sadness for me, a revenge.

Chapter Three
Evidence into Action

The question is whether EIAI is more about how I established an international reputation as an incisive critic of public policy or how Colin and I teamed up to change the world.

Walked to the Tiergarten and entered opposite the Brandesburg Gate. It takes me over thirty minutes to walk. I vary the route. Andrea bikes everywhere and cannot understand why I walk. Walking is the same as thinking for me. It is autumn everywhere. Autumn feels more northerly here. Starker shadows. Greater contrast between light and dark. There are less shades of contrast between them. More northerly here than London, I mean. I don't know if that is geographically correct. I sat in the Tiergarten. Not too far in, because I become anxious. At least I can always hear the cars. Another reason not to cycle in the centre of Berlin. Too many cars driven too quickly. Then the anxiety on the U and S Bahn. Is it bigger than the London tube? It feels roary, hostile, the trains bearing down on the passengers like large angry predators. I think of the old-fashioned dinosaur skeletons that greet me when I visit the Natural History Museum here. Because more quaint, somehow more convincing than in its opposite number in South Kensington. Makes me think of children, of Noah, of Neil and of sadness.

In the Tiergarten, I see a jay. I didn't even know there were jays in Germany. Why wouldn't there be? Perhaps I was mistaken. It flew low and fast from a tree branch into some bushes. Flashes of orange and blue, it is a large bird. The colours reminded me of seeing a kingfisher with Neil. It was abroad somewhere very hot.

The Tiergarten jay, imagined or not, takes me to Tooting Common. I was with Colin. We were walking on the common.

It was a Saturday, I think, a weekend at any rate. I had just said I had not seen a jay for ever such a long time and then he pointed at it. Sitting in the branch of a large oak tree, it perched as if to say here I am. It didn't move. We watched it. Colin explained it was a type of crow, a predator. He would know. That would have been the kind of thing I would have said to him.

I am trying to remember what time of year it was. Are jays seen more at one time of the year than another, to do with their breeding or feeding habits perhaps? I have no idea. I cannot remember what I was wearing in our walk on the common that day. The walks were infrequent enough, so it was unlikely to have been cold or rainy except that I liked, still like, to walk in the increasing coldness of autumn ahead of winter. You do get real snow in Berlin, unlike London most years. No snow in the forecast here yet.

I have struggled with the chronology of the three years of EIAI. I know it ran from the year after the book's publication, that is from 1986 to 1989. Within that timeframe, I cannot remember or find out when it started and how the events of those two years unfolded. Even the meeting with Graham, the conference in Birmingham, the approach there by Colin and our subsequent meetings in Mayfair. Most of the documents from the time are destroyed. I never keep diaries. I know most of the records from EIAI were physically destroyed as I shredded them myself towards the end. I didn't want to leave a trace and now, searching, can hardly find any. Mentions in the newspapers, such as I can find, are far fewer than I had thought at the time. It is as if EIAI had never existed. Is it different now with the internet or are our fond projects equally vulnerable to obscurity?

Colin took our affair very seriously. He rented a flat in Tooting. I insisted on paying half. He did not understand why as he would have preferred to pay. I still at that point attempted to explain what struck me as obvious in terms of power dynamics and identity. He listened politely as we sat in the kitchen in the one bed flat on the first floor of an interwar terraced house let to us by Mr Gupta. I was grateful for Tooting. It was cheap. The motive was Colin's fear of being seen by someone he knew. He thought this unlikely in Tooting.

The flat was furnished, and Colin insisted on adding his own touches. We sat in the kitchen with a red and white oilcloth

29

tablecloth on a bistro style round metal table he had acquired with matching bright red metal foldaway chairs. He bought a CD player and a VCR and expensive Egyptian cotton sheets and covers for the brand new duck feather duvet. Each time he came, he brought an addition. Some quite earthy ceramics in dark browns and blacks, new crockery with a Japanese style decoration and a pink ceramic lamp with an aluminium shade. He bought wooden hangers for the wardrobe where he would carefully hang his beautiful hand-made suits before we made love.

The walk on Tooting Common was an indulgence. I think he enjoyed it as much as I did. Yet his fear of being seen, of his private life with his family being irretrievably compromised meant this was an indoor relationship. He was pleased with himself for spotting the jay. I quizzed him gently on his fears of being found out, and he replied they were simply rational. Like the firm, he boiled everything down to what would work on the basis that the challenge was to solve the problem and that everything could be solved. There were no loose ends. When I suggested that Tooting Common may not be so safe as it was probably where his colleagues came to buy sex, he didn't laugh, just suggested we went back to the flat. Even now I am surprised he was never mugged. This was only a few years after the riots that had spread as far as Tooting High Street. It was not safe for a man who appeared from the tube in expensive hand-made suits carrying a leather case from Libertys. Maybe he had assessed that risk and made the necessary arrangements. How would he explain being in the Tooting vicinity when he was mugged. Buying special ingredients for his Indian cookery, I expect.

I think we were Mr Gupta's perfect tenants. We used the flat solely for sex and the blossoming of our indoor relationship, paid the rent promptly and sorted out various long-term plumbing and electrical problems at no charge.

EIAI provided two things for me—two things in addition to the love of Colin. I found out about government and my academic work was given the perfect amplifier in the wider international dimension of think tankery and political quangos. I now realise I exaggerate with the confidence of a 30 year old living in the chaos of not needing to choose any consistent position on any particular issue. I think now that this was the natural stepping stone to Stefan who would allow me the same sense of multi polarity, of not being pindownable, and make me understand where my ideas, my interpretation of the academic material presented to me there and then, could take us.

I celebrated my thirtieth birthday, I mean on the actual day of the birthday, with Neil. The picnic was on Parliament Hill Fields. Bagels with delicious vegetarian fillings, hand made by Neil that same morning plus two delicious salads and fruits and fruit juice. We sat on the hill, eating and drinking. Neil was in his own sober mood. He wanted to understand, that is what he would have said, why I wanted to work on EIAI. Before I could he started to answer that, he got it about being a great opportunity and that I was in charge and the great salary. I kissed him. I wanted to say, trust me, because I didn't know really either, except it expanded the possibilities.

The following weekend in Tooting on the oilcloth tablecloth, Colin had laid out lots of expensive Greek dips with pitta breads he explained were freshly made in a Greek bakers he knew served with stuffed olives, sun dried tomato salad, stuffed vine leaves and Champagne. A neatly wrapped present waited beside the food and drink goodies. He watched for my reaction. I didn't disappoint and didn't want to. The present turned out to be an antique, decorative silver bowl, for what, I still can't fathom, but I still have it. Colin pointed out its utility as something we could share in the flat. And he asked me if there was someone else for me too.

At which point my snide recriminations about Colin's need for secrecy, for complete discretion, crashed down around me as broken pieces of my own hypocrisy. I actually gulped back tears. I was ashamed, even though Colin assured me it was ok. It was symmetrical. That was the term he used. Symmetry as fairness, the reason I paid half the rent, but symmetry as delusion. Loving Colin became so important to me, is so important to me, yet I married Neil not so long afterwards and genuinely thought to devote myself to monogamy in a way alien to my previous existence.

When I sit in the Tiergarten, I try to remember and when I remember to organise in some way, first chronologically, then conceptually and then in terms of happiness—mine or others'— what the hell has been going on. To write this up—for that is

31

what these sessions at Andrea's kitchen table increasingly feel like they are becoming—provokes a feeling of incessant creativity as well as lingering futility. Is all our work to write up the world a creative fiction of ourselves that Colin or Neil or others would never recognise? Perhaps my concerns over Colin's confidentiality and privacy are overdone.

I console myself now with the reflection that love, the genuine feeling of desire and overwhelming protectiveness, I felt towards men has served also to mask my own needs tacit and explicit. Colin provided me with the perfect entrée to a world for my own advancement on my terms. Neil enabled me to explore, examine and exhaust any desire for family. That is the story of my emotional thirties. The really interesting parts all happen later. Did I know this then, sitting on Parliament Hill Fields with a man wooing me as best he could while wondering how could I of all people have joined the firm? Looking intently at the jay on Tooting Common with the man I loved before he explained fairness was about the symmetry of lies.

"With this in mind then, the thought that science as commonly understood—especially science in the area of medicine—provides, fuels the public's belief with a system of understanding perceived as objective and rational. It is the task of the political system to mould ideas that fit with an ideology and with a scientific rationale that creates the possibility for the exercise of power, especially within the checked system of democracy. That is why public policy in our age yearns to share its bed with the likes of the economist or the social scientist. Perhaps truer to say, first the economist as social science, and more lately with the unleashing of capitalism as a scientific certainty, the economics of capitalism itself. The fixed points of the firmament of political thinking have never more than now been anchored in the quasi-religious academic dress of science rather than on the surer ground of inherited characteristics of power and rights. The right to control our resources has been fundamentally overturned by the power of the scientifically charged state to make us do its bidding in an age of certainty. The NHS and the nationalised industries of the UK have first demonstrated this power.

Now, with the science of state monopoly and control, including through the NHS the extension of the state's control over our own minds and bodies, we have not abandoned the need for a scientifically credible and objective rationale for public policy. Instead we have simply created a new set of scientific realities—the power of the market, maximising utilities, the power of trade—all conveniently located in the interests of a post-colonial need for dominance. Hence the importance of the counter proof— communism and the Soviet Union—in associating with an iron bond national security with the legitimacy of scientifically rigorous public policy. There is no alternative. The politics of make-believe."

It is extraordinary to find the 1987 speech on today's internet. In 1987 somebody had actually videoed me making that speech as I spoke on behalf of EIAI at a conference in Rome. The video had somehow survived and now was free for anyone to see who googled Stella Kelly and EIAI. It is in fact listed fifth on what is an incomplete and rather short list of references to my first foray into public life.

It sounds dated in its references to communism, the Soviet Union, nationalisation. I had not realised how heavily influenced we all still were by the 70s. Much less rationale than a response to a time that seemed nationally hopeless. I dealt with it, I remember, by ignoring it, by looking forward. Listening to myself, I was living in a long, unacknowledged shadow. The shadow that has cast a veil of scepticism over even the scepticism that has become my academic tool of choice.

I am so young. The bob. The Next suit. My body still defined as much by childhood as by maturity. We think of ourselves as adults, yet even at thirty, we are still playing at an attempt to be the adult that only experience can fashion from the essentials of our character, our idiosyncrasies or fears and blunders. I was so confident.

My instinct is to show Andrea. Then I am afraid. What has happened to that confident, over-confident young woman genuinely on the cusp of the successful career I have led? Where is Colin? He is not on the podium with the speakers as I confidently project my ideas to some collection of government and other senior people. They all look twice my age. I am not that person anymore, and it makes me think I never was, not really. I remember the event because of being in Rome. I remember it as one of a series. They are not marked by anything of emotional or personal significance. That is what has changed. Then it was all about making my way, about my work, about creating a sense of self-importance. I had a secretary who travelled with me. She had back up from the office at the firm. We took taxis from airports to hotels. Ate meals on the go in club class airport lounges. It was a performance, and I was the star.

Now how I feel gets top billing. I never want to give another lecture. I have stopped writing my next great work—*Providence, Not Progress*—to write this memoir of questionable taste or purpose. It is a work whose quality in terms of style, structure and content is already marred by inconsistency and a halting unwillingness to avoid the sentimental in interpreting the personal with a vivid sense of personal vindication and sadness.

I have to show it to Andrea. We have an openness between us that is so joyful. It is not a risk. She will love my thirty-year-old self even if I appal her. We have no secrets. She has not yet read this manuscript. She will be the first person to read it. She does not yet know about it. She believes I am writing *Providence, Not Progress*. That is not completely untrue. Only the draft of that work lies untouched in a file on my hard drive. I have not looked at the research and background material for some time. Andrea does not intrude. I have made it a condition that I need to have finished my book before she may read it. I mean this book, but she believes the other. Or at least wait until I have reached a stage given my health, where I believe it is sufficiently finished. It will not help to read it bit by bit like someone inspecting the partially finished panels of knitting instead of assessing the finished garment.

I watch the video again. It has had over thirty thousand hits. I don't know whether that is a lot. It sounds like a lot. I search Stella Kelly and the *Politics of Make-Believe*. The same video link comes up as number fifteen on the list. So perhaps other academics look at it or students or voyeurs trying to come to terms with the eighties the way my generation tried to come to terms with the fifties.

I have been looking for Colin, for the young, so to speak, forty something man I was having an affair with. Of course, he was not there. He was always in the background, pulling the strings. We saw each other at weekends when possible or evenings, in the Tooting flat. We were not a couple. He would leave. We spent a few hours a week together at most, and only occasionally, would he stay over. He worked hard himself. He was constantly meeting contacts, making contacts, introductions. Money just seemed to arrive at the firm from these not always obviously commercial activities until you realised that for Colin and his contacts, the meetings, the discussions, the introductions were the money making activities that most clearly and insidiously translated the money spent with the firm into the currency of power.

As I had been looking for Colin, I had missed Mary. There she was, sitting at the table of guest speakers on the podium, listening politely to me—she often shared these platforms with me. That is how I remember her. Intent and intelligent and one of a small number of people I had counted on in building EIAI.

I met her at the firm and that should have been sufficient warning. It was in the first few months of setting up EIAI, when it was still not decided what kind of government quango was being created. She worked for a charity—what we now call an NGO—with an expertise in public policy in the Commonwealth. The Commonwealth was still something you talked about then, and her charity had a long history of support from Commonwealth countries. Its original brief had been to support missionary activity, and somehow, it had successfully changed into a key support mechanism for nascent post-colonial governments. Mary was quite straightforward about the way it worked. Our involvement is a condition of support and alignment with UK Government. The work was closely aligned with Overseas Development Agency and the Export Credit Guarantee Department. Enough said. Mary was very supportive of EIAI.

There is no way of telling from the video where the event took place, except for occasional announcements in Italian. Otherwise, it is all in English. I guess if you watched it, you would guess it was somewhere in Italy—the Uscita notices in the lecture hall, the odd Italian announcement—but nothing to say it was Rome. I only know it was Rome, because I remember the event, and I remember it distinctly from the others precisely because Mary was there. Although I failed to see her as I looked vainly for Colin, I must have known she was there because of our excursion and the decision to invite Mary as a key advisor in setting up EIAI.

Mary had suggested staying an extra day. I checked back with the office. They were unsurprised. Why would they be, as I had time in my schedule. I phoned Colin who was equally supportive. Told me I had earned a break, why not make it a couple of days. So we did, Mary and I, tagging it on to a weekend and giving me an unexpected break, a holiday in fact.

Mary took charge. She knew the city really well, and I felt overawed by her comprehensive account of its ancient and renaissance history. I believe I was meant to be. We visited galleries, museums and monuments. Mary was selective as I explained. I easily tired of endless pictures—especially religious pictures—and a little went a long way. She suggested various restaurants that were all superb. We drank, but not a great deal, an aperitif and a glass of excellent wine with each meal. The weather was gorgeous—spring, I think, as it was sunny but not overwhelmingly hot.

Mary asked me how this compared with my academic life, and I was forced to admit that it didn't compare—they were two different animals. Mary smiled. She was always even humoured—with everyone, I think. As we sat in the still warm but now darkening evening having a coffee after our meal eaten outside, she told me that she trusted me. I was an outsider to this world and that gave her the confidence to unfold her own struggles to conform.

Those were, as best as I can recall, the types of words she used. I was looking into a reflection of my own constantly nagging doubts. But it was a reflection that I avoided most of the time because of my decision to embrace the firm's world in its entirety if I was properly to understand it. That would be food and drink, literally, for another time.

Perhaps it is too much to ask you to indulge my thirty something self, but these contradictory emotions of needing to conform and a sensed disloyalty to a personal ethos are the common place of how we move from young adults to mature and less-illusioned beings. I do not think now that the money, the travel expenses and lifestyle are a bribe. They are simply the necessary consequence of allying yourself with the powerful and authoritative. When you step away from that alignment, resources also fall away. I might add that in these years, I began to receive Christmas cards from my Vice-Chancellor just as the government research grants propped up his university's social science department. There was no question in my academic world that the price I was paying was a fair one.

Mary said she had reached the crisis point where she felt compelled to choose between her beliefs, a personal need to support humanity as if it were an endangered species and her work that she saw as compromising the fundamental human rights. It is funny playing back in my head how this conversation must have sounded in the relative late night quiet of the pavement restaurant. Looked at it now, the answer is so simple. There is no conflict. You can only express your own personal values through the existing systems of power and authority. If you challenge them, you are taken down.

But that was then, and I was enchanted by this reflection provided by Mary's moral quandary. Instead of the dark and murky shadow that had persecuted me and I had refused to acknowledge, Mary brought into the light of day a golden view of how and why we needed to establish EIAI as the counter within the system, the opportunity at least to see things in an alternative way where belief counted and those who controlled science could be challenged. Is that even remotely true?

Andrea is back. I hear her key in the lock turn, and my heart leaps a little. Even now, when someone we love returns, it is a moment of such joy. Yet I am anxious. I want to show her the video, but I fear her response. She will not be angry or negative towards me. She has too much love for that. Somehow I fear she will feel let down as I do a little. I need her forgiveness to allow me to forgive my younger self.

We eat a simple dinner. Andrea, without needing any discussion, has recognised my fragile appetite. Some lightly steamed vegetables in a broth of Thai style spices works perfectly for me. I contrast it in my mind with those Roman dinners with Mary.

After dinner, I take my camomile tea and we relax, still at the dining table—the same table where even now I am writing this part of the memoir. I explain about the video on YouTube, and Andrea is keen to see it. She immediately picks up on my anxiety and is quick to re-assure me. We laugh as she compares these videos with the pictures we have of our childhood and the fashions that now inevitably look clumsy and over the top. She understands that the past is a dangerous territory to travel in, and she knows I am extinguishing some ghosts I have met along the way.

The video lasts fifteen, twenty minutes. Andrea watches it in silence, and I watch Andrea. She smiles. She is my enchanting and enchanted friend and companion that make these last months tolerable. After it has finished, I tell her about Mary. I tell her that Mary convinced me to trust her. That I did and I also responded to Mary's need for a resolution to her perceived ethical conflict. I offered her a job at EIAI, and she took it. From then on, it became a two-person project. At that point, I lost control of how it would unfold. Andrea gently points out that I never had control. Control belonged to Colin, who belonged to the firm, who belonged to the government, which belonged to the system of power we are all powerless to change and always trying to change like flotsam washing up on the beach or the psychotic patient lecturing the air.

I know all of this, and I knew it then. I trusted Mary. I was at school, and I was befriended by another girl, Wendy. I was so pleased. I enjoyed having a best friend, of being singled out. We became bosom buddies all through our last four years in school, until we went to university. Then we lost contact. I wrote to her in my last year at university, but never heard back. I went around to where she lived, where I had often spent afternoons and evenings, and her parents explained she was off abroad doing something. So the friendship had been a temporary affair, but not for me, and to this day, I feel so let down, so abused. It was the same all over again with Mary.

In the Berlin flat in the German autumn, more autumnal now, Andrea comforts me. Here where I have alighted an injured animal, a confused passenger looking for the correct exit for my eventual destination, I experience the comfort of Andrea's knowledge. Now that is an emotional tonic for a run-down academic—to be enveloped in knowledge. The comfortable knowledge I adhere to, my very own little corner of make-believe.

The Politics of Make-Believe is still taught in our universities, but now as a component of how systems of critical thinking were revised and reinterpreted in the context of a new neo-liberal consensus that rejected the permissive optimism of the sixties as jejune and politically dangerously inane. I disagree. The part of the book that never made it into EIAI was the second half of the thesis. If belief trumps science in the development of public policy, then the science upon which belief is founded in a modern age is itself weighted in favour of the prejudices and programmatic priorities of the factions most able to exploit the system to gain and retain power. More straightforwardly, science secures resources to explore only areas that are aligned with the power system it serves which in turn requires the make-believe that, for example, medical science extends everyone's life (whether or not that life is especially worth living) or technology creates weapons that secure the safety of people (especially after two massive European wars) or that landing on the moon will make us all proud of being part of the system that poured resources into these various political goals. That is what science helps us all to believe in.

Chapter Four
Stefan Selbst

In 1989, I handed over the directorship of EIAI to Mary. Everyone was very polite and proper about the decision. I do not think they were delighted. I had lasted less than three years in the role—although the agency was well established internationally. I needed genuinely to return to my academic studies. I felt I was unable to achieve the academic goals alongside the hurly burly of government and its quangos and advisers. There was an unspoken sense of betrayal, I felt, especially from colleagues at the firm.

In 1989, the Berlin Wall fell along with communist East Germany. My decision and that geopolitically momentous event were unrelated except chronologically. Yet with the benefit of hindsight, a double-edged telescope of memory, they appear to me a crossing point between my personal life and the generation to which I belong. We are the blessed ones. Never having to pay for our education, our pensions, our health care. If we made it to university, we could expect well-paid jobs and had a good chance of health into an unprecedented old age. It doesn't work for everyone, but history will look back at us as the blessed in a golden age of peace and extraordinary conciliation. These prizes are slowly being taken away. The laurels fade.

When I first spoke to Stefan, he gave me the confidence to be bold, comprehensive and contradictory. His art unleashed possibilities in my narrowly focused academic role that before I had not imagined possible. My response was, of course, *The Illusion of Government*, the post-cold war volume that has done so much to undermine the concept of Western democratic government as an achievable—desirable—goal for all nations on the planet.

1995, I visit Berlin for the first time. I am there to lecture at an international conference on the post-communist opportunity for Europe. We were being hosted by the Berlin School of Society and Life Studies. Like many Berlin institutions, they were intent on getting an international presence. Funding for these kind of events never seemed to be a problem. Maybe my old friends at the firm were helping with their special funding mechanisms. It didn't bother me too much, still doesn't. There is a limit to ethical horizons where government is involved, whatever type of government you wish to designate.

I never got to give the lecture. We were seated at the front of the hall with maybe 100 or a few more in the audience in some expectation. As the chair for the day rose to speak, people in balaclavas came into the hall. They had loud hailers and sirens which they sounded. Some started to use spray cans to create slogans on the off-white concrete walls of the lecture theatre. Three men, who appeared to be the leaders of the gang, made it to the stage and took off their masks. I noticed a couple of people with video cameras who were recording what was going on. The slogans and the loud hailers made clear that we were now part of an artistic event. We were being re-created.

The audience was largely a group of academics, like myself, who shared certain views. We challenged each other, but we did not take part in demonstrations. I felt, I remember very clearly for once, a sense of shame that we did not take part. We had been taken by surprise, caught at our own game. We were once again nothing more than a part of the system we pretended to analyse, understand and explain—if anyone was listening. I was captivated and decided immediately to delay my paper. I wanted to incorporate this artistic event into what I wanted to say. I didn't want to be in a traditional lecture hall in an institution keen on re-asserting its place in an order of things momentarily derailed by Soviet communism. I found a part of myself.

The event lasted for about 30 minutes. Although some security staff did arrive from the university, they were stand offish and tolerant of what they maybe saw as a prank. Some of the academics were indignant. The chair, rather unexpectedly, embraced the affair, inviting the leaders of the creative event to speak to us and explain what was going on. He was sadly not quite able to bring order back to the chaos. The creative event contained its own meaning—we should have guessed that. So instead of explanations and the nice nasty conflict of academic debate where the personal is thinly concealed in the theoretical, we took a break for coffee.

Meeting Stefan the next day when I ducked out of the rest of the conference with a bogus bout of food poisoning felt in every way like being a badly behaved schoolgirl. I lied about my sickness to get out of doing a lecture I no longer wanted to do and letting the organisers down. I was meeting someone who possibly enthralled me, but who many colleagues the previous day had condemned as a childish prankster. I was anxiously uncertain of how to engage in conversation with the inaugurator of creative events without appearing like a boring, out of touch university lecturer. This sense of teenage apprehension failed, as so often in real life, to take into account Stefan's own complete sense of dominance, importance and self-confidence. I realised immediately when we started to speak, when he told my enthralled self that he had read and admired *The Politics of Make-Believe*, that he would assume I would want to know him. He would determine whether I was worth knowing. The opposite was outside his perception and imagination.

The teenage comparison is a good one in the clumsy way his own vulnerability, his knowledge that the whole artistic enterprise around which he had begun to build his reputation rested primarily on an outrageously exaggerated sense of self-worth and artistic value, constantly sucked the sand from under his feet like a retreating wave. I was able so quickly to read and understand this situation despite him being the best part of ten years my senior. So I could join in his conditioned emotional state while observing wryly how we grew a rapid graft of association and need. I don't know how clearly Stefan could have articulated this rapid acceleration of our mutual acceptance and belief. He made clear that in his creative events, I held potential to advertise, invent and subvert. It was an agenda that corresponded equally to the emotional and intellectual needs that meant my sense of purpose had ended.

He lived in a dirt, cheap and poorly furnished flat on the east side off the iconic Bernauer Strasse. Here was where he had his studio or the events management company as he dubbed it. The studio—the management company—was the living room of the flat, empty of permanent furniture where his co-workers brought the items they were working on—banners, costumes and disguises, life size objects like musical instruments, sewing machines, radios. These were either real or look alike models. Usually the objects would be broken and smashed up. There were tripods for the numerous photos and videos needed to create the events. His bedroom was equally untidy and communal alongside another room with a couch in it used by visitors to stay overnight and a kitchen minimally equipped to support his workforce.

He invited me there after our first meeting. He liked to drink coffee and smoke cigarettes—he died after all of lung cancer. I never smoked and disliked the smoke heavy atmosphere of the place. I wanted to talk to him. I wasn't interested in the process of making, of creating, and he often criticised me severely for this failure to enter into and understand his world; how he constructed my world. But this was later.

In 1995, when he literally burst into my world, he represented the open door I was seeking to exit my life. Andrea understands and explains correctly, in my view, that this was the first time I was able to connect myself as a conscious adult with a life experience of which I wished to be a part. This is how I connect the fall of the Berlin Wall with my departure from EIAI in 1989 with a creative arts statement at an out of the way academic conference in Berlin in 1995.

I didn't want to hang out with Stefan in his nicotine fumigator. I used an excuse. I wanted him to explain Berlin to me in terms of sense of place—politically, historically, geographically. So we needed to walk, and everywhere we walked, there was this wonderful sense of anticipation, possibility and barely contained apprehension. This was before the now familiar redevelopments had happened. It was the fertile ground of a city's topography where the imagination saw the future as only beautiful. A dream like all dreams that has diminished as the concrete has been poured, and the old and new cities jostled and replaced the east west divide.

It is the ending of autumn. Much colder, the trees are bare, and we are all wearing our heaviest coats, scarfs and gloves. It is a moment we can enjoy as north Europeans, with our Christmas preparations and markets. Berlin glints with wealth, power and confidence. It is now so different. Yes, I believe the dreams have mainly come true. I have run here as if to paradise. Andrea officiates.

It is the evening after the video of the Rome conference. Andrea continues unmoved by my embarrassment along with my need for her to see this earlier version of myself. She is re-assuring. I have not changed, yes, I have changed. She laughs. In so far as I want to be different, so have I changed. In essence, always we are the same. We cannot be changed and we should not wish to. Let us grow instead.

On her way to the university she was crossing the road at some traffic lights. She tells me with pleasure about the experience. Everyone started to cross, as Germans do, when the signal turned to green. It was busy in the rush hour. Andrea saw a phone fall to the ground. She wasn't sure, but thought it had fallen out of the coat pocket of a woman walking towards her. She had called out and startled the woman. Andrea had pointed and another woman walking behind the woman who had dropped the phone scooped it up from the ground and gave it to her. "Vielen Dank, vielen dank," the woman had said to Andrea.

Andrea still effused joy from this tiny interaction. For her it summed up and contradicted the mood of pessimism and conflict fostered by 24 news. It was her anecdote and antidote. She smiled, laughed as she repeated the story. Not just Andrea noticing the woman had dropped the phone, but the other woman working in tandem to recover and return it. The woman's surprise, the woman who had dropped the phone, that she was being helped; that because of these strangers, her day had been rescued from enormous inconvenience.

I should like to speak to Andrea about Stefan. From time to time, when I first arrived here, I would gently touch on the artist. Andrea would change the subject. Start talking about the sexualisation of art in the renaissance and its influence on the likes of Andy Warhol. There were many possible reasons for these gentle deflections. They had fought, which was not Andrea's style but almost a must for Stefan. She disliked his openly aggressive stance on issues. He would suddenly change sides during an argument, or take a different, perverse position. He would argue with ferocity for the destruction of the art establishment on one day and the next argue it was a fundamental part of the subversion of meaning in the art it endorsed for the benefit of producers and owners alike. She had known Stefan before I had, when he first arrived from the East as soon as the wall had fallen. Andrea had embraced him, and this was her equivalent to my Rome lecture rubbish. Like me she had believed. Unlike me, Stefan had continued to exert an influence as an artist famous now in his own right. She had been tricked; part of his trickery, the world's trickery.

Perhaps also, she continued to grieve for him. She had organised his funeral. Difficult, as he had left no instructions. To everyone's dismay, but I was not surprised, he had also become an icon of unity Germany; as the artist who summed up memory as voiceless. I want to ask Andrea how she thinks Stefan would now react to the video of my EIAI conference speech. That is another possibility for her reticence in speaking of him. How irritating it must be to have her opinions, ideas, views constantly contrasted with Stefan's posthumous outlook. Especially since, to be true to Stefan, such views would need to be as contrary as they were in real life.

We eat the lentil soup and homemade (bread machine) bread Andrea has prepared. I tell her about my walk in the crisp, dry cold. We both enjoy these days. Andrea repeats yet again her delight over the mobile phone story. We both laugh. Andrea is concerned the soup is not really enough for me. It appears it is for her, so why not me I ask. I know she is really asking about my health. Am I eating enough? I have never eaten much, I explain. This appears to satisfy her for now. However, she is right. My appetite continues to be a problem. Along with this, the tiredness increases as do the varying manifestations of anxiety that afflict me.

I tell her I am thinking about referring to Stefan in my writing. She doesn't pursue the topic. She asks me instead how *Providence, Not Progress* is going. I say I am pleased with it, meaning this memoir. So far, so good. She likes that expression. So English. I laugh. We both laugh. It is a joyous evening. *Memoir* has been fused with *Providence, Not Progress*. I do not feel I am being intentionally dishonest.

If Andrea will not help me discuss Stefan in the context of my writing, let me introduce how she acted when Stefan and I first began our walks together. She warned me about him. Not as

45

a sexual predator—which he was. She knew I would make my own decisions about that. He wasn't, I thought, after me sexually except to subject me. That would not be allowed. Those were my terms, and if he rejected me as a fellow traveller, so be it. The warning was an odd combination of concern about his East Germanness and his artistic folly.

Andrea successfully walked a difficult tightrope between the demands of a leading German university and the necessity of remaining internationally credible as a leading theorist of artistic sociological thought. For her Stefan would always be primarily an artist, a practitioner—for him too, I think. For Stefan, Andrea would always be first and foremost an art critic, only secondarily an academic. They required each other as part of an intellectual and artistic system. However, at a personal level—sexually, intellectually, emotionally—they would remain hostile and suspicious, precisely because they could see sufficiently into each other's souls to be appalled.

I think it was this complexity of reasoning that led Andrea to invite me to apply for a post as visiting professor at the Berlin School of Society and Life Studies, where she was a department head. Yet, I must stress, that it was, as I have said, Stefan, who inspired the writing of my *Illusion of Government*, the book that ended the fallow period after the publication of *The Politics of Make-Believe* ten years previously in the mid-eighties. It also corresponded with the divorce from Neil and the separation from Noah that still fuels his resentment for me, his adopted mother.

Stefan used me as some sort of catalyst for his artistry. Most people thought we were sleeping together. Neither of us did anything to dissuade them. It was simpler that way. For Stefan, it would have been out of character to be able to spend time with a woman unless there was a sexual element. He needed people to believe this was consistent otherwise he would be admitting a woman to a position of influence which for him amounted to vulnerability. For me, that was a price worth paying with the added benefit that it kept other men's attentions to a minimum. It was all in retrospect very alpha male. It was important to me that Andrea knew this was not a sexual relationship. She did accept this, but I knew that she believed I had failed to heed her warning. It did not jeopardise my distinguished visiting chair and has had no lasting impact on our relationship. It was never in any way on her part about jealousy. She accepted my sexuality and got on with her own life. Andrea, as you probably by now have realised, is built for happiness and blossoms through the happiness of other people. She would never have wished to blight the happiness of how Stefan and I tackled the world.

We met at the Hauptbahnhof in Berlin. Of course, this was 1995, ten years before the new station opened. We were going to Dresden. I try and work out the time of year and fail. I cannot recall the weather or anything topographical about the day. I remember the station and getting on a really old fashioned former East German train with individual compartment and sliding doors off a corridor down the coach—the sorts of train carriages I grew up with and had all but disappeared by the time I went to university. The train, I remember, because as well as being old fashioned was so slow. Stefan was smiling. I remember his face floating in the air inside one of the compartments wearing this elaborate smile. It told me I was being given an inside tour of the old East Germany. I didn't need much imagination to fill in the gaps.

Dresden itself was this odd assortment of the laminated concrete of post war rebuilding—cheap and ugly, buildings like the cathedral still smashed by the war itself and remarkably, beautiful if grubby palaces and churches that defied the communist need to thrust utilitarianism as progress into the populace's face. Stefan wanted to show me the art gallery and the wonderful collection of old masters it possesses. This is why he had become an artist.

All the time we were on the train, and when we were walking in Dresden and in the gallery itself, Stefan carried an A5 sketchbook. It had blank but quite heavy-duty paper. The leaves were fixed using a metal spiral so that they could be turned right over and the sketchpad used as a makeshift drawing board. Stefan told me right from the start that he needed to be always changing his art—the ideas, the focus, the audience and more importantly, the media and means of delivery. The *Create Events* happenings through which we had met had already been franchised to someone else in the colony he effectively led. I thought he would use the sketchpad for drawing. Instead he would write on each page (later, these books have commanded ridiculous amounts at auction). The writing would itself take many forms—but always handwritten. He would write tiny paragraphs in biro or large, single words and phrases in marker pen. He would use comic book blobs for thoughts and speech. Block capitals for aphorisms. What most concerned him on our trip to Dresden was his East German past and how that memorialised the future. What could be the artistic implications and possibilities that were now released as knowable in this suddenly uncertain and unknowable future? If you spent 40 years living in East Germany, not knowing with any certainty what the future held was a new form of trauma. It was apparently the direct opposite of the trauma of the mono, knowing of East German society and the terror of the state.

So what I will attempt to do—and I want to do this as a form of personal testament to Stefan—is to set out in my words what I think made his art specific, personal and wonderful. It is a very personal set of views. If I am shot down—I hope not by Andrea—but more likely by an academic establishment that has occupied this territory, so be it. In this I am only willing (slightly) to relent to an alternative view that rubbishes my own on the grounds that I am not German, and to that extent, have no business having any views at all.

The word most often to appear in Stefan's sketchpad was voice—or voiceless. He was shifting. That is what he said. He was shifting in response to the shift he had experienced with the end of the East. He spoke at length to me in Dresden on this topic. Remember, this was in 1995, only six years after the wall had come down. There was nothing yet in Dresden to match the life we were used to in the west. There were bars thick with cigarette smoke. Cafes were thin on the ground, and the best you could hope for were greasy chips and overcooked, unsalvageable veg. That was on a good day. Stefan laughed that even sausage was limited in quantity and terrible in quality. Here you might as well be a vegetarian. Now, when you visit, it is so different. Imagine a place without salad.

In the evenings, we would drink beer in the smoke filled bars. During the day, we would walk, spending time outside unless we were in the gallery. We must have walked miles. Always Stefan carried the sketchpad. Always taking notes as we talked. I think he talked and I listened. I interrupted him with questions. This he welcomed. He would pause. Sometimes the question was going to lead nowhere so he just ignored it or said it was unhelpful. Often he would pause and change tack in his conversations.

Perhaps the reason why I don't remember the seasons or the weather or any particulars of our walks and talks—other than the gallery and the dreary sense of place of a post East Dresden—is that Stefan took me to an alternative East Germany. It contained the bad food, old railway carriages with compartments and sliding doors, the assemblage of tacky post war concrete buildings and uncleaned, uncared for baroque grandeur. Stefan's East Germany was a more imagined thing, it was what he wanted to contain through his art.

If art contains the sense of past and the possibility of being, Stefan believed that art had been extinguished in the lifetime he had spent before the wall came down. He had expected that art, in his then he admitted very limited understanding of it, would be released by the acts of 1989. These were the creative events. The spoils of a freedom that could defecate on the liberal twoddle imported by well meaning (or not) economic missionaries from the so-called developed world of democracy and freedom.

His disappointment bordered disillusion. It came with the anger and embarrassment of anyone whose belief has been proved false. He was simply let down. Let down by his own artistic naivety. He acknowledged that one reason I interested him was because I had foreseen this in *Make-Believe*. He had read it but still failed to apply it to how he would experience the end of the East. His disorientation was grounded in the impossibility of being able to rehearse in advance for these political events—reunification was a word he avoided—these big changes that ought to signify for him a release but instead made optimism less hopeful. He was still at a stage of being one of those Soviet refuseniks who turned up in the west in the 70s only to criticise their new hosts more severely than the Soviet Union. After all, the Soviet Union had history on its side. No one there had ever had the opportunities squandered in the west.

I remember this particular day—not the weather but a specific event on the day. We were walking by the river when Stefan wanted to stop for a coffee. Unlike now, that was not an easy need to meet. Cafes did not alternate shops along thronged boulevards and precincts. They were tiny, below ground affairs.

We knew one that we had used before and made our way there. Stefan was agitated. Smoked two cigarettes in quick succession en route. He knew I disliked him smoking indoors when we were eating or drinking so he would go outside. He wanted to talk over a coffee. We reached the café and were the only customers. You went down some steps to the semi-basement room with four square tables and hard stools instead of chairs. We were served two coffees, freshly made on the stove as we were the only guests, and there was no point in keeping coffee brewed. I asked for milk. There was none.

Stefan started to tear the pages out of his sketchbook. He placed them face up on the table. Then, running out of table-top, he pulled two of the other tables next to the one where were sitting. The person serving in the shop (its owner?) began to take an interest. Were we expecting friends? Stefan indicated not by shaking his head. He was busy working with the pages from the sketchbook. It was a puzzle or a word game. The shop person continued to be interested, pulling over the final table as Stefan was running out of space again. He refilled our coffee cups with the rest of the newly brewed coffee. There was a sense of excitement.

In the centre were the voice/voiceless sheets. These spiralled out like a snail, the words becoming smaller and less distinct. Some of the smaller words in biro turned out to be squiggles, hieroglyph lookalikes. There were real little sketches, and I recognised some of the creatures from the tiled palace in the Pergamon. Then, separated by empty table space, were the sketchbook pages containing the paragraphs of script. The man serving appeared to understand. Stefan and he were laughing.

It was the man serving who explained it all. This was how people attempted to communicate and cover their tracks in the East. You wrote on separate pieces of blank paper that were left around the place. Artists like Stefan would reassemble them and attempt to make sense of what the individuals wanted to say. However, as it was too dangerous to have an opinion, none of the individual pages could ever on its own or with other scraps provide a coherent statement. That was the statement. That was the art. The art of the voiceless. Almost conspiratorially, we drank more coffee, the man serving now joining us at our table as we admired Stefan's work—his art, his creation.

By now, of course, you will have recognised the work I am referring to. It has pride of place in the Hamburger Bahnhof. The tables, their instantly datable red Formica tops and chrome trimmings, pulled together loosely with three chairs beside them. On top the random or ordered depending on your critical perspective sketchbook papers (the very ones!) and against the stark white wall behind a slide show of the individual sheets with a key showing where each lies in relation to the others. The title, *Individualisation*, and a brief curator's note, "This is Stefan Selbst beautiful recreation of the act of reunification."

Sure it is. But then the good people of the Hamburger Bahnhof need to tread wearily to ensure their artworks remain within a broadly western tradition of progress and insight; a testament to the ability of the west to see through itself with humour and candour. Andrea begrudgingly adores Stefan's *Individualisation*. She has a more pertinent commentary as someone who admires Stefan's work, was appalled by his sexual politics and arranged his funeral and the testimonial lectures that are now a foundation text in her subject.

I have my own views. They are personal. I believe, probably incorrectly, that as I was at the point the work was created—over the period of its creation when Stefan and I were working in some kind of tandem—that I have a unique insight. Although he called the work *Individualisation*, the words at the centre that alternate irregularly and sometimes together are 'voice' and 'voiceless'. Sometimes we have 'voice-less'; 'voice(less)'; (voice)less. For me Stefan is telling us that the western individual is as disappointing as the voiceless citizen of Dresden. I would go further and say that a reason for the success of his art in the west is the connection he is able to make emotionally, I would say artistically, between the terrorised suppression of dissent in the old east and its subversion by the politics of individualisation in the west. It is a comedy, and this he did say as we were leaving Dresden, that Marx would have understood this well.

Stefan's reputation changed when *Individualisation* was shown for the first time. He moved from the East's most famous artist and became part of his generation's pantheon of world artists recognised, exhibited and purchased all over the western art world. He became as at home in Chicago and San Francisco as in Berlin. I do not know if he visited Dresden again. His fame was accompanied by wealth, and he became instrumental in the new Berlin. His death in 2010 at the age of 53 was reported globally. Dying at a relatively young age only enhanced a reputation, and his limited and often ephemeral art works are highly sought by contemporary galleries across the world. It remains something of a scandal that to date Tate Modern has missed out.

Andrea is home again. She is cooking some beautiful dishes in the kitchen. The gentle aroma suggest we shall be having Thai food for dinner. I wonder if she really knows what I am writing.

1995, when I met Stefan Selbst and came to Berlin for the first time. When I conceived the possibility of *The Illusion of Government* and accepted the honorary chair Andrea somehow managed to create for me.

Chapter Five
Family

It is difficult, writing a memoir, to observe religiously a chronological principle. I apologise. I needed to write about Stefan so that I could express and you could understand how the opportunity opened for me in Berlin in 1995 to move there and write, in less than a year, *The Illusion of Government*. Now I must fill in the missing years. Berlin is the door that opens those years.

When I handed the directorship of EIAI to Mary in 1989 I was ready to return full time to academic life. Academic life, however, was not quite so ready for my return. My time out meant I had lost my way in the jostling and positioning that accompanies academic careers. I was welcomed as I had been a conduit for research funding. I was treated with care but also with suspicion. My hidden agenda was to take up my studies again, but ascribed to me were all the ambitions for advancement characteristic of the colleagues I had, to use their term, left behind.

I was now tainted because of my association with the firm and with the Tory government of the time. I used this to my advantage. I considered it as part of my academic practice; that I was not entirely steeped in that version of reality. My book reinforced this hybrid, for some a little exotic, for others diseased. Colin made sure the grants did not dry up. Colin told me before I had handed EIAI over to Mary that she had made a pass at him. I asked him why he had turned it down. She was attractive. He had grimaced. That had made me feel good.

I married Neil in 1990, the year my dad died. The wedding was a registrar office affair with a couple of friends, one of them was Mary, as witnesses. We thought of making more of it, but we were both busy and didn't really see the point. His family was a bit aggrieved, I think. I had little or nothing to do with them. My family were for me already something in the past, something I had escaped.

My dad, the slipper-beating monster of my childhood, had not improved during my remaining time in the family home. I left as often as I could as a child and teenager. University provided the definitive opportunity to cut ties. Some social history. It is difficult to over-emphasise the social impact of the student grant. I got paid to go to university. I could supplement this by earning money. I was economically independent while still able to study full time. Because I have never needed much money and because that money has always been reasonably easily available, the independence I always craved was mine at 18.

To begin with, my mum had attempted to maintain contact. She sent letters, never more than two sides, in which she detailed what she and my dad had been doing. He was taking early retirement (my student grant went up). They were worried about having enough money. They were thinking of moving somewhere cheaper to live, smaller, near the sea. They had had a pub lunch while looking for somewhere new to live. They had not heard from my brother, had I? She sent the occasional present: some cheap cosmetics, a book token to help with my studies. I never replied, and the letters petered out after a couple of terms.

My brother had been equally quick off the mark. He left to qualify as an accountant and also did not look back. None of us were estranged exactly. None of us felt the need to be in regular contact. I missed my brother's wedding—he never invited me. My mum was invited, she told me, but refused to go unless my dad were invited as well. When she told me, I applauded my brother's resolve. She went anyway, on her own, as I knew (and so did he) she would.

Mary was appalled when I described this situation to her. I hadn't thought much of it, but when she came to the wedding ceremony, she queried why there was no family. Neil did look abashed and said something about wanting to have a quiet wedding—nothing fancy. I would need to ask him more later about that version of the event. I was not up for the same level of evasion.

When Mary learnt at the pleasant restaurant where the four of us—our witnesses and ourselves—celebrated after the wedding, she was aghast. She could not understand how I was not in touch with any family members. She went on about Christmas and explained she spoke to her mum frequently, and I think she meant pretty much daily.

I did not want to be smug about my independence. I felt, still feel, it was a measure of my success. I had no desire to be part of this group that had made my childhood dreary, frightening. Mary's comments did prompt me to call my mum—I would put the phone down if my dad answered. The phone line had been disconnected. When I rang my brother, he did reply. They never told me they had moved—to the coast—as my mum had written about years before. I wondered how Mary would respond if her parents moved without letting her know. My brother asked what had prompted me to ring. I evaded the question, thanking him for letting me know. There was a silence at the end of the phone. I didn't like to ring off without some formal conclusion.

It was Winston who persuaded me to come to my dad's funeral. He said the move to the coast had only made things worse. What could I know of my parents' years together having left as soon as possible? Winston said he had kept in touch on and off. There had been little encouragement. It was the truth of my mum's life that by backing my dad she had forced a wedge between herself, us, her friends such as they were. That continued on the coast. I imagined their dull days, the grey, cold, rainy moments when she, more alone than ever, cooked for my dad, cleaned their ground floor flat, washed and ironed. How had she and I ever had anything worth talking about, worth keeping in touch for? He said he had kept in touch to give her a bit of moral support, because he felt someone ought to—not barbed at me, I think. I ran.

He did persuade me to go down on the slow, ghastly, broken down train from Victoria to the little settlement on the northeast Kent coast they had chosen. It was a grey day, drizzling, so becoming for the funeral of an abusive, useless father and husband. I still remember and imagine all their days, coastal and suburban, in that same grey, drizzly none place. They weren't even puzzled. Moments of apparent pleasure—a trip, a party, a drink—were, I estimated, the main event. I walked from the station, about 20 minutes, Winston gave me the directions. The station, like their block of flats, was some way from the coast, so I never even saw any sea. It was a street that could have been anywhere but was my dad's and therefore my mum's dream of retirement. The ground floor flat, what they could afford and put some money in the bank—my dad would have liked that—had a single bedroom that contained the same double bed they had slept in since their marriage, since before I put them in the family way. Now that time seems so long ago. It seemed an apparently different age even back then—1990—now itself ancient history. Bloody, dead thank god Margaret Thatcher the terrible.

Arriving at the front door, I rang the bell. An older woman I did not know opened it. I started to enter with the old instinct of familial possession. She didn't bar the way. She just stood in it—not comprehending. I remember telling her, by way of explanation, I was my mum's daughter. I remember the reply, "I didn't know she had a daughter."

My immediate reaction was to make a run for it. I had been erased—success! How stupid of me to let my brother win his argument that I would regret it (how—unspecified) if I didn't turn up for the brute's funeral. I owed it to my mum. Even as the chance to turn and run occurred to me, it evaporated as the woman showed me into the gloomy lounge. She was saying she was a neighbour, from upstairs on the second floor, as I saw my mum, head turning towards me, looking. She mumbled something and returned her gaze to the floor, hands clasped together in front of her, her elbows on her knees. She crouched, expecting something, not to pounce but to be pounced on, expecting the next event. The next event was the hearse pulling up outside. There was a black car provided for the mourners. Mum, my brother, the neighbour and me. We all wore traditional black. It wasn't sad, it was absence and acceptance. If there was an emotion, I would call it relief. He wasn't going to be missed. Not even by my mum.

We waited outside the crematorium for the previous funeral to finish, while the funeral director explained we could use the waiting room if we were cold and that we needed to adhere strictly to our thirty-minute slot as it was a busy day. His gallows humour was wasted. There was no danger of overrunning. Taped music began and ended a brief farewell with somebody nobody knew making some remarks on the man in the coffin which, he claimed, followed conversations with Winston and my mum. There wasn't much to say about my dad—loyal, hard-working, family man. Nothing about the beatings, the abuse of my mother, his objections to my vegetarianism. I realised on the train home, nothing about me.

I was expecting the coffin to disappear behind the curtains, but it was wheeled around the side out of sight. The funeral director—as we filed out and probably grateful that we had got through in only 20 minutes—explained the crematorium had broken down the day before so the body would need to be taken to a neighbouring one in the next town. I remembered the winter of discontent that had brought Thatcher to Downing Street in 1979 and the misreports of the dead blocking mortuaries because of strikes by council workers. I was glad Colin could not see my origins.

I had no idea where we were. I had just joined in with the ceremonials. The funeral car could have brought us anywhere. Now the funeral was over, I wanted to get away. We all headed back towards the black car. The man driving it kindly agreed to drop me back at the station on the way to my mum's. I waved as I stepped out, mumbling something or other as Winston said couldn't I stay in a rather needy way. I couldn't. It was a cold wait of over an hour for the train back to Victoria. It was a cold, unnecessary return and reminder. I felt nothing at all, except cold.

Winston rang a few days later. He wanted to meet. A post mortem, I suggested. He didn't laugh or register the inappropriateness of the phrase. We met in a pub. Winston had become a successful man. He was everything my dad hadn't been. He showed me pictures of his wife and two children. He spoke of them with joy and was equally animated speaking about his job working in sales. He even tried to sell me a pension. I liked him. For two hours, we spoke freely, mainly about ourselves. He was interested in my work and very open and winning as he admitted he could not imagine what it took to write a book. Just so, I could not imagine what it took to sell whatever he sold, anything, even ideas. He said he would look out for Mum, but she was her own worst enemy. He wanted to be friends, so we were. From a distance, we remain friends. We meet some years. We let each other know when we move house or change our mobile numbers. Yet I haven't told him I am dying. We're not that close. Mum was still alive, he told me, last time we spoke.

I married Neil, because I was 33, successful and imagined it was time to settle down. I married Neil, because I envied my brother's happiness with his photos of his wife and children. I married Neil, because I was frightened by the emptiness I found in my mum when I went to my dad's funeral. I don't know exactly why I married Neil. He asked me, and I said yes, and we got on with it. I spoke to Andrea about it this evening. We have moved on from the discussion of my performance in the EIAI video clip. How could it have been that I loathed Thatcher so much at my dad's funeral, yet worked contentedly—passionately—at EIAI established to prop up her regime by Colin and the firm. I don't discuss that with Andrea. Absurdly, I was about to say that there is no such alienation of right and left in German politics when the truth is that German politics lives in denial and eschews such violence as part of an errant history. Which is more dangerous, benign disbelief or rampant expressionism.

I discuss with Andrea why I married Neil, because she has been such a big support for my leaving him so many years before. She is clear—and I really welcome her clear thinking—that I married him because of the expectations brain washed into me for my whole life. I argue back. Me! How could I have succumbed, the author of *Make-Believe*. Yet she is convincing that just because I could describe the trap of belief didn't mean I could avoid it.

When I told Colin I was engaged to Neil, he congratulated me and asked if that meant we would not sleep together anymore. He asked in the way you might ask if we could no longer have lunch on Wednesdays. That was because sleeping with me had become, at least for me, rather like a regular lunch date. The main difference, as with a tennis match, was the need to undress and shower afterwards. I remember kissing him and saying I didn't expect it to make much difference. Colin looked pleased, shocked and disapproving. That, at least, is how I think he responded. The Colin I was now very fond of would have responded in that way.

In reality, marrying Neil precluded much sexual liaison with Colin for practical reasons. Lunch was definitely much easier and fun. The Tooting flat became superfluous to our needs and after a final stay there—I had to lie to Neil that I was teaching on a residential course for the firm—we gave it up. It was a moment of sadness. Colin, I believe, missed the frisson of an affair, although I think he was relieved that he no longer had to endure the anxiety of being found out. He remained at the firm doing what he did. This included introducing me to various people in and around Whitehall. I continued to feel slightly in awe of these networks only a little later concluding that I was just as much part of and equal to the other characters in the network. More make-believe. How could I miss it? Colin and the firm reimbursed me by speaking and teaching invitations that were well paid. The university smiled on this, telling me I could legitimately keep the earnings as relating to grant raising activities—honest graft it was. It also kept me away from competing for the academic promotions my colleagues craved. I remained at the rank of senior lecturer. My book continued to be required reading not just for undergraduates but for budding politicians and civil servants. Is it normal not to notice when you are a great success?

Andrea asked me about how I was last night. Honestly, I don't really know. She wanted to know about my writing, so I began to tell her about *Providence, Not Progress*. I don't talk about my memoir. I don't tell her that I have put *Providence, Not Progress* on hold, because I need to write this right now. I don't know why I don't tell her. I am not ashamed of this work. In my mind today, during this Berlin sojourn, it is more important than the academic, quasi-academic lots of people would say, stuff. I'm glad Andrea asks me. I shall think about telling her about my memoir. For now, I just continue to tell her about *Providence, Not Progress* as I don't think there is really very much distance except style between the two works. All of my work has really been about seeing through myself, and this is so much easier in the past than the present.

I asked Andrea how long might I stay. She lifted her arms as if to say it did not matter. Then, uncharacteristically, she put those same arms right around me. We stood together, her holding me, for a while. It was so comforting. I didn't move until she finally released her gentle hold. Then I felt like I was going to fall down. We were standing in the vestibule, I can't remember why, when we had this conversation and then the embrace. I moved into the sitting room and staggered into a chair. I felt myself collapsing inwards. Andrea followed me into the room. She sat in the other armchair like we were a married couple. I thought of her partner—she had left since I can't remember, a long time. I thought finally of broaching that subject with Andrea but knew it was not welcomed. She would tell me at some point, or maybe not.

The intensity of love I feel from Andrea, of being wanted, of not needing to do anything particular to deserve this elevates me even now as I write about it. I believe I can stay here forever. Andrea and I can breakfast together and when she has gone to the university, I can sit at the kitchen table and continue my memoir. I still go out. It is much colder now. Winter is beginning, and I had forgotten how much colder winter is in Berlin than London. Because I am older, I feel the cold more, and I am more fearful that I will catch a cold. I eat oranges every day to stave off illness. When you are dying, there is more point to maintaining your health than in the humdrum everyday life I used to have.

When we sat in the armchairs after Andrea's beautiful, warm embrace, I asked her if she minded me telling her about my health—how I was feeling. She acquiesced. I love her so much for accepting my dying self, my accelerated dying that the medical profession prefers to ignore. The doctors do not believe me, and I do not believe them or their tests and diagnostics and prognoses. In telling Andrea, I make the events as I am experiencing them much more real. They stop being thoughts about how I am feeling and become facts. That is how facts happen. Because they are spoken. I do not think facts happen when they are written. That is just a textbook version. Facts happen when you speak them to someone, when you speak with an active emotion. For Andrea, this was love. For some, it is hate. For my dad, I think, he spoke facts with hate like, "Stella, you will never make much of yourself, especially if you continue to refuse to eat meat"; "Stella, it is rude to your mother not to eat meat"; "Stella, you will only have bread and water unless you eat meat." Those are facts, facts of my childhood now

60

remembered, now thinking about his death, his funeral, leaving my mother in the back of the funeral car when I asked the driver to drop me at the station. Not going back to that flat. Not speaking with my mother, without emotion, without facts, without the fact of herself. Erasing that fact. Forgetting the facts of childhood for as long as I can.

I didn't speak to Andrea of that, of what I am writing in my memoir. I told her about the anxiety. She wanted to know if there was some trigger for the anxiety. Was it to do with my dying? Was my dying to do with my fear of dying, so that by accelerating in my mind the idea of my death I could pre-empt or take control of an event of its nature outside my will? As we sat, me folded into myself in the two armchairs in her living room, her questions sounded distant or meant for someone else. I explained the anxiety. It happened most extremely when I stood on the platform of the U or S Bahn or on any train platform. I felt this surge of anxiety that I would fall off the platform or in front of the train. It meant I tended to avoid using the U Bahn. It also meant I used it more, just to go one stop, to challenge my anxiety and prove to myself I could overcome it. My worst stations were the Hauptbahnhof and Ostkreuz. The height and the depth were how my fear felt to me.

Andrea listened carefully. I could feel her mind assessing how to respond best to what I had said. She knew that her questions before had been too technical, too analytical. I carried on speaking. I wanted to provide her with more information. I told her about how the anxiety, most obviously prompted by walking on the train platform, surfaced at other times. In the Tiergarten, when I walked outside, it was not then a fear of falling off the platform. It was something with the symptoms of a sickness, nausea and a blinding headache. Andrea listened, and there were no more questions or embraces. She held me in her presence. I still feel held this morning. It is so comforting. Thank you, Andrea.

I felt very moved by what I wrote this morning about Andrea. I was so settled, I decided to take the long walk over to the Tiergarten—to risk it. I was right to do this. Now, returned, I feel more whole. There was no anxiety and no need to take a train to test my resolve. It is too cold now to sit outside in the Tiergarten, so I walked over to the new—that is post 1989—shopping precinct they have built where dead man's land used to be beside the wall. This is strident, confident, capitalist West Germany in the ascendant. Like every new building, it is full of glass verticals and long escalators. I took one today to the first floor to test my nerves. So far so good. I go to a café and order an Americano, without milk. It is brought to my table. As I sip it, I notice a group of people arrive. They have come for lunch and are dressed festively. Of course, all the shops are decorated for Christmas. It is December, although I had largely ignored this. They are in their thirties. They are having a work Christmas party. I am intrigued. What do they do for a living? They seem pleased to be out together and exchange gifts that make them laugh. I can remember doing this too, but not for some time. There is a thoughtless pleasure of those years when I just worked, for the firm, for the university, a thoughtlessness that is simply not noticing what is going on in the way now I do and must do all the time.

I hope I am respecting the chronological approach specifically. I am one of those people who get lost easily in films and novels that play around with time frames. It takes me half the film to realise it started in the present, and now we are somewhere much earlier in the characters' lives. It keeps my feet on the ground to remember what is happening now. Andrea's kindness. My plight and state of mind. It helps me to see the past better. The experience of the past is itself not chronological. I can easily recall periods of time, events from those periods simultaneously from childhood, early adulthood, later in my life. They do merge, like a film, into a story that seems continuous but happens in the wrong order. That is why I hope you have forgiven me for jumping ahead in the previous chapter to my first meetings with Stefan.

I see the years between handing over the *Evidence into Action Institute* to Mary and meeting Stefan and then moving to live here as a fallow period. In my life, I made what others would describe as momentous decisions. I moved back into academia, all be it keeping one foot in the world of the firm. I married. We adopted our son, Noah. The sexual relationship with Colin ended to be replaced by a more rational, intellectual companionship. In so many ways, this was satisfactory. I was approved of, by the university authorities, by Colin and the firm, even, if I had enquired, by my own family or at least Winston, my brother. I lectured—undergrads as well as the excellently remunerated conferences and training courses largely put my way by the firm. I certainly believed that I was making a useful contribution intellectually and especially in the way public policy was developed internationally.

It was certainly true that my reputation rested on the twin pillars of *The Politics of Make-Believe* and leading an innovative government agency. That certainly gave me a unique appeal. I played that to every advantage. It was odd that I failed to notice the absence of any growth in my own thinking, of what came next, the doors my work and experience could open.

That is why I need to see it through Stefan's eyes. In Dresden where Stefan created *Individualisation,* I stopped. What he taught me to see was the possibility of ideas as a visual presentation of meaning. By his use of physical objects, in his working methods and in the eventual artworks—none of which I believe was ever finished, all a work under development, in motion, insubstantial—he transformed the object into a description of our lives, an inversion within which simple articles of everyday existence summed up the lived lives of people—all sorts of people. For himself (for Selbst!) that was, I am so sure, completely tied up in his experience before and after the fall of the wall. The discovery, although that is too sudden a term, (exposure?) that the longed for life in the west—freedom, summed up in the newspapers he always insisted on reading and rewriting in his work—could only disappoint as the previous life of lies startled and degraded. His reply, to use illusion as a means of visual reality, startled the art world itself into reappraising the use of illusion for so many centuries as the basis of intellectual understanding and knowledge.

This was the intellectual journey I made with Stefan in Dresden in 1995. It is what led to the outpouring of unrestrained intellectual endeavour that resulted in *The Illusion of Government*, my second major work, written in just a few months immediately following my appointment to an honorary Chair at Andrea's university and my move to live in Berlin for the first time. No wonder Berlin is the place where I feel safest.

The great wonder for me about *Illusion*, invisible to outsiders as it is not discussed in the book because it lacks any academic purpose or rationale, is the illusions I most exposed were in my own life. The illusion, fostered relentlessly by everyone during the fallow years. The illusions of my five years of marriage, of the supposed joy of adopting Noah, of my so called intellectual companionship with Colin, of the rounds of lectures where Stefan had woken me from this trance of contentment—of illusion.

I am pleased that *The Illusion of Government* was such a success. It appeared to be perfectly timed as the sequel to *Make-Believe,* and the two books are strongly related, with *Illusion* being a deliberate progression of the first work. If politics requires the magic of *make-believe* to acquire power, then to maintain power, governments require the illusion that they are powerful, in charge and able, benignly or tyrannically, to impose their will. It was so simple. It was, beautifully, universal as the many examples I used began to prove. Of course, like all universal proposals, its weakness was in exceptions, but even here, as a conceptual approach, it offered the get out of any illusion would itself be governed by the make-believe it built upon. When we stop believing, the illusion is shattered.

Indulge me another time as I step out of the chronology of my memoir. It is 1997, two years after I have moved to Berlin and the Dresden trip with Stefan. I am excited and apprehensive. *Illusion* is to be published. I have invited Stefan and Andrea to read the book in advance of its publication. I have not asked them to critique the book—perhaps I should, but I wanted, as I explained to them and I think it was true—I wanted to rely on the colder, impersonal supervision of editors and academics much more likely to deride and attack what I had to say. Always best to see off the criticism beforehand. I have surrounded Stefan and Andrea's reading of the book with a little ritual. It is two days before publication, and we are back in Dresden for two nights. We arrive at the end of the day. I give them each a printed copy of the book, and they have the evening and the following morning to read it. We will meet on the afternoon of for me to receive their initial reactions. I explain I want this to be as raw, as immediate as possible—not considered or rationalised.

Stefan applauds my plan. He wants to video the afternoon session—a suggestion I reject—as part of a future artwork.

Andrea opens the session. She is deeply appreciative. It is her style to be scholarly. She is gently positive of the range of references I have drawn upon and the originality and quality of the argument. It is, she says, exemplative of that quality that I say something apparently obvious that is deeply hidden from view. Hidden, she suggests, because of the subversiveness of what I propose to power. To challenge power from the academy is a dangerous undertaking.

Stefan is listening politely. He nods. He agrees. He tells us both he wants to respond differently. He starts to write on his sketchpad, as ever carried with him. He gave me the pages. He was right. It was the death of my dad that made illusion a possibility, just as the death of communism made it an impossibility for him. But I jump ahead. We are not in 1997, we are in 1990. My dad has died. I have married Neil.

Chapter Six
Neil and Noah

Noah has emailed about Neil. He attempts to sound unconcerned, but is clearly upset. Neil is now in a wheelchair to get about. He can manage in the house with crutches and has moved to live on the ground floor. Noah has moved back into the house. I can't believe they are still living in the same house—two up two down—that we bought in Tooting (for my own old time's sake) when we married. I can't really imagine how Neil manages to wash. There used to be a tiny toilet under the stairs. Otherwise the only option is to use the basin in the kitchen. I don't know why this bothers me of all things. I expect the whole house has been renovated. I can't remember the last time I visited, or even if I did after I had fled to Berlin the first time.

I never felt properly a mother. We fostered and somehow Noah stayed on. He was and is bright. That was unusual. We broke most rules, but in 1990, people seemed less upset by that. When we married, we were both keen to do something for humanity. That was also more usual then. Thatcherism didn't really contaminate values until she had departed. Then it was still normal to want to make a contribution to society. We ended up as foster parents by accident, because Neil knew someone at the council, and they were running a campaign to recruit foster parents. We were assessed, had a trial run. That all took most of a year. It was madness when I think about it now. Yet, we were both successful. Neil in the less pressurised job. Noah turned up in 1991, aged 12. He and Neil immediately got on. Noah stayed.

The idea of fostering appealed to me, because it was temporary. As I saw it, Neil and I had temporary charge of a child, generally an adolescent, to give them a chance of some alternative future, a place to think. Most of our fostering experience was difficult. I mean the children were difficult. That is what made Noah special. He was not difficult, sullen, angry or violent. He did not smoke or drink or do drugs. When Neil started to teach him how to get something out of school, how to learn, I suppose, he responded. He achieved educationally. I think that is why the social workers left us alone. They could see we were getting a result. With Noah in pretty permanent residence, we withdrew from further fostering. Noah was happy. He used our surname, although he was never formally adopted. Neil and he adored each other, and, I presume, still do.

I failed to notice that we had become a family. We breakfasted. Neil would drive to his work at the lab, dropping Noah off at school on the way. My work was less regulated. I would be the one who was away quite often, staying overnight. In the early nineties, there weren't all the ways we now have of keeping in touch, so my time with Noah tended to be concentrated in short spells—outings at the weekend or holidays. Neil encouraged me to spend time with Noah. He wanted me to share the strong bond he had built with the boy. That never happened. Noah did not warm to me. He was never vocal about his feelings. All the same I knew. I even think he resented me taking him away from Neil whom he relied on completely with a trust that never failed him. I could never compete with Neil. At some level, Noah despised what I did, or what he thought I did, as lacking seriousness. No, I didn't work in a laboratory, I didn't do clever maths, I couldn't explain scientific stuff. And Noah was simply not interested in politics or history or the kind of science I practised. He looked through it as empty, meaningless. He made me doubt myself, even as I felt myself divided by Neil's constant attention—their constant attention for each other.

We holidayed in Provence one year. I guess it must have been 1994 or perhaps the preceding year. Noah had established himself in our home, for Neil as a son, for me as an unpaying guest. We drove down there. The journey was lengthy, and we were tired by the time we broke our drive staying in Beaune. Noah had been his usual quiet and thoughtful self on the journey. We planned to go and choose a restaurant for dinner and sampling some wine. However, Noah asked permission to rest and read in the hotel. We thought he liked the hotel. It was a novelty, and we felt he would be fine by himself. He must have been 14 or 15 at this time.

Neil ate steak in the restaurant we chose, close to the market on a winding, narrow street. French picturesque or kitsch, we were enchanted. The food was simple and perfect. It was not too rich, and I was able to eat a goat's cheese salad. I never found it a problem being a vegetarian in France for all that people tell me. We ordered and drank a bottle of quite pricey wine. It was suitably delicious. Neil had his back to the window of the restaurant, and I was facing him, looking out across the street. It was still light and warm when I noticed Noah. He was outside, loitering and watching us. I managed not to catch his eye and hoped he had not seen me watching him watching us. I wondered why he was doing this. Clearly, he had decided not to remain reading in the hotel. Perhaps he was bored or hungry. Yet I decided not to speak to Neil about it or to look again to see if he was still there. I thought I would ask him later on, casually. Why had he come to find us if he didn't want to join us.

This was the holiday, these 14 days, where we played this game of who was part of the family and who was not. In Arles, I was keen to see all the Van Gogh sites. We bought a typed photocopied sheet from the tourist office. It was makeshift with what appeared to be a hand drawn map, providing the locations of the famous pictures. When I said we could spend the afternoon walking around the individual sites of the pictures, Noah insisted instead on visiting the Roman amphitheatre with Neil. The triangle of the three of us constantly eluded me. Neil said I was imagining it. We all had different interests. He preferred, he said to visit the amphitheatre. It was too hot to trail around after a few old sites which looked much better in Van Gogh's paintings any way.

By the time we reached Aix where we were staying in a rented gite for the second of our two weeks, the pattern of Neil and myself dining alone had been established. I encouraged Noah to come with us. He had brought a large number of trashy novels to which he seemed addicted. Neil said to leave him, not to hassle him. Noah listened, obedient yet defiant. Even now I distrust whether I am right in perceiving the defiance, mistaking it for my own sense of rejection. Yet, I am sure he wanted to push me away. I loved picnics and wanted to shop in Aix before driving into the beautiful countryside for a lazy picnic lunch. The weather was beautiful—so hot, so sunny. Instead, Noah and Neil had planned to take the train into Marseille and explore the port. There was talk of a boat trip, fishing. I arranged to be dropped in Aix where we parked the car. I would walk out to Cezanne's house by myself. Have my own solitary picnic.

The walk to Cezanne's house was ill judged. It was uphill and a bit further than I had imagined. Although the house itself was quaint, the walk was through modern apartment blocks along a tarmacked road with a high wall that prevented any view of Monte Sainte Victoire along the way. My supposed idyllic stroll was tiring and unrewarding. Now I think about it, I felt similarly disappointed by the Van Gogh sites in Arles. This was not like me. I had momentarily bought into the idea of family life, with Noah and Neil, but it was not working, it was not happening as it was supposed to. I retraced my steps back down the hill into Aix. I had already abandoned the idea of a picnic. What was the point when you are by yourself? I sat in a café on the main square with a coffee and a pastry.

We decided to attempt the drive back to the ferry from Aix in one go. It meant we could spend an extra day in the south and we could both take turns driving so that although it would take us over 12 hours, it could be done. I didn't want another night in a hotel with Noah spying on us. Neil thought my concerns very overdone. He reasoned that this was Noah growing up, practising being independent from us. Yet he had been left to his own devices for much of his childhood with poor parenting and different adults looking after him in various homes. Why would he need to practise being independent. He needed to practise belonging.

When I asked Mary to be a witness at the registry office wedding with Neil, she asked me why I was marrying him. It was a Mary question. The thing that made Mary successful, the ability to conceal in the everyday a thoughtful analysis. She hadn't meant the question as a pleasantry, but that is how I had treated it at the time, and as a result, it had continued unanswered into the marriage itself. Specifically, now it was the question that Noah did not ask but always, when I saw him, I knew needed to be answered. He did not think me good enough for Neil or maybe for himself. I felt judged. I was judged. I failed to measure up.

Now it takes me so long to compose a sentence. The thoughtfulness required and the disappointment, usually, with the subsequent result, is pitiful. Contrast that with how I was then. Then I worked so fast. I had the confidence that comes from the need to get the stuff out and done. That is how I imagine it. This cannot be correct, because I am describing my fallow years. I am describing the years between EIAI and my rebirth at the hands of Stefan in Berlin. Those years, 1989 to 1995, were empty of any extension of my thinking, of the ideas that modelled and enabled my early breakthroughs and success. I do not remember thinking of it like that at the time. This later making sense, or storytelling, is fine but inadequate to describe precisely how those years were in the moment. That is mostly lost. The pace, I think, the extreme pace I have described in the assemblage and blurting out of my thoughts was replaced for five or six years by a different pace. It was the pace of things, the pace of family, the need to keep up with an idea always alien to me that there was a purpose and meaning on the raising of children and partnership beyond a willed companionship of friendship.

As I circle around these events, I can touch the feelings surfacing once again in me that are always invoked. Invoked by the spectacle of photographs, still then religiously laid out in photo albums, edited highlights, edited at least of the story of family. In these photos, I am always active. I am putting out picnic things, applauding at some sports event or other, making decorations for a school event. I am joining in with a frantic aspect of determined glee. That I don't remember. In the photos, where there is Neil, there is Noah. They are the true companions. They strike poses of heroism, athleticism, enthusiasm and hilarity. Their lives are enacted in the photo albums I now recall, and I am there to act, to do, to make, to let them lead their lives. That seems to me now to have been the deal then.

I do not agree with Andrea that they were the authors of my desertion, my flight to Berlin as it turned out to be in the end. I had never fitted into my role and the pace of all those family things overwhelmed my personal compass. If there were a true north for me, too much interference confused and abused it during those years.

I think the Provence trip must have been 1994, because it was in the following summer that Noah and I fought openly. It was the summer holidays, that flashpoint of change for every child that marks the annual progression to what's next. Noah wanted to go to Brighton for a day. We watched the weather seeking a day when it would be fine, and I would be in the country. Neil thought it was a great idea the two of us should spend a day out together. He knew he and Noah were the main event—not intentionally but just how it had turned out. He wanted me to have more of a share of what was for him such an intense, personal and emotional bond. Brighton sounded fine to me. We agreed, at my request, to a picnic—my favourite as always. We would picnic on the South Downs, somewhere from where we could see the sea.

The day arrived. Noah brought one of his novels. I think he was reading thrillers set in the Second World War. I disapproved and kept my disapproval to myself. I was inclined to ask him why Brighton and did so while I drove us down the motorway there. He seemed uncertain and was open in his confusion. First, the sea, he thought would be good. He had read *Brighton Rock* at school and wondered how much of that Brighton survived. He wanted to see the racecourse. He had never been to a racecourse, just seen them on television. There was something about Brighton, I surmised, that met his needs for the slightly exotic and edgy tinged with the possibilities of adult life—personal choice, wrong choice, pleasure—the things that he was still thinking about and worrying about actually getting into.

It was an ominous note that I missed. For the first time, I felt I was being allowed in, allowed to get to know this alien child that had landed on our doorstep five years before and taken over Neil. Yes, taken away, I think was how I framed it to myself privately, privately even from Neil. What I should have seen, and shied away from, was danger. Instead I thought I was on to something and foolishly kept my course through the day.

The weather was fine. We parked in the multi storey near the front and walked along the promenade. It was hot enough for ice creams. We arrived quite early, but soon there were crowds of summer day-trippers drawn by the sea and the lovely weather. Noah appeared in good form. He was enjoying his ice cream. The pebbles put him off the beach. Not mentioned, or he hadn't noticed if they were, by Graham Greene. He had imagined sand. He started to speak about the Provence holiday. He told me how much he had enjoyed our trip to France the previous summer. How much he had liked the towns, large and small, across

Provence and the food, mostly, especially my special picnics. He became quite specific about things like the tablecloth, the picnic hamper and wicker basket we used to carry food and utensils in. The pottery plates we had bought from a local potter and used until one had become broken and we had reverted to the plastic ones we brought from home because we wanted at least two of the pottery ones to make it back home. He had a precise eye for detail. He lured me in. I was amazed by his sensitivity a year later to all the touches that mattered to me; that I did not even know he had noticed. How could all of this have been happening and me unaware?

A year is a long time in a child's life. One summer compared with another so I asked him about this summer when our holiday plans were incomplete, partly why we were having a day out like this. He said he understood. I think, buried in that, was an attempt to say he didn't mind, an unimplied criticism, that I was at the heart of the problem. My commitments were such that I could not easily surrender two or three weeks to a proper family summer holiday. He could have gone on to say, as I did to myself, that there were benefits. He could see more of Neil as they were able to go off together at any time. He could be careful about how he spent time with me. Brighton was, after all, his idea.

We stopped in a little Italian café just behind the front for a coffee. I saw across the table for the first time the adult Noah in waiting. I was in every way surprised. He was assured and filled the space immediately around him with a quiet confidence that provided an impenetrable defence from criticism or bullying. He also physically looked like a younger version of Neil. He was becoming Neil's progeny, right there in front of me. The self-assuredness that marked his whole posture slipped once he began to speak again, but now I had seen it, I knew it would come to be how he managed in the world.

He was talking about exams, about what he wished to study. He had made his mind up to become a lawyer. He wanted to go to a good university, study there and then qualify. He asked me what I thought, for approval not for discussion and I duly approved. Do I make this stuff up? As he sipped his coffee and discussed his future solemnly as young men do (now he is a young man, but he was only 15 or so) what I heard was criticism of me. He did not choose to rate or use my connections, my knowledge, my network. He implicitly rejected my world. I bit my tongue. Why was he being so foolish? I was a powerful woman. It meant nothing to him or he had failed to notice it or he had chosen to reject it and make his own way.

Rather abruptly as I recall, I suggested we take the car up to the Downs and find a spot for lunch before it became too crowded. He paused with his new and unnerving self-assurance indicating he had not finished his coffee. He was right. His cup was half full. Clumsy impoliteness on my part, his gesture meant to me. He drank it quickly and stood ready to go.

We drove to the racecourse. There was now a thin filter of cloud drifting across the sky from the sea. No threat of rain to mar our picnic plans. It provided a welcome respite from the intensity of a midday sun. Noah compared this English summer day with the intensity of the summer days in Provence. He spoke with a calm insistence on the benefit of dissimilarity and the balance of a comparison in which judgement was suspended in awe of the wonders of both. Law sounded like a good option, I remember thinking. If they're not your own, children's talents can threaten and overwhelm your identity. Perhaps they can if they are your own. That didn't matter, because the definition of my relationship with Noah—this is what I realised as we stood beside Brighton Racecourse—was as an adopter not a mother. I did not feel I was his mother or wanted to be, and he knew it. Like me, we both knew I had never wanted to be.

There were picnickers in lay-bys beside the road, but I wanted no traffic, and we drove away from the racecourse towards Beachy Head. We parked at a random point along the coast road and walked over the open ground towards the cliff edge before selecting a spot where we spread the large throw we used as a groundsheet and put out our provisions. We were now alone, and the sea could be heard but not seen, breaking on the foot of the nearby cliffs. The light cloud continued to provide us with sufficient shelter from the sun for it all to be pleasant.

I have blocked out the details of what happened next. I do not want to remember and cannot remember. It was as if I had pursued the boy. I do remember how I felt. How I wanted physically to throw him off the cliff to his death, to pursue and hound him to its edge so that he would fall. I was in the grip of an anger that our arguments and words could not contain or express. I don't remember him showing fear. Quite the reverse. He displayed a patience of someone who had long expected and prepared for my naked show of aggression, of hatred it would be fair to say.

The picnic was ruined. I ordered Noah back to the car. He calmly obeyed my instruction. I was the one out of control. I threw together the picnic things into the boot. Noah sat silent in the front seat. He had no words for me; no condemnation, forgiveness, no attempt whatsoever to relate to me. Why did I feel both bitter contempt for myself and the need to be thanked by Noah not forgiven? If it was about forgiveness, then I needed to forgive myself. So my rage did not abate but boiled over into what Neil described as the unforgiveable act.

We drove back to Brighton, and I parked on the front. I ordered the boy out telling him he was going to the station. I gave him money. I told him I didn't want to drive him home. He must find his own way. I saw him walk off. I didn't know or care whether he knew where to find the station.

Neil was at home. He looked upset. Noah had rung him from a friend's house, where he had gone after coming back on the train. I had to leave. Noah would not return to the house if I was in it. Neil backed him.

Today it has been very cold. I am waiting for Andrea to return so that we can eat dinner together. I have made my version of lentil soup. I know she likes this. It is flavoured with tomatoes and chilli powder. She finds the piquancy of the chilli very British. That is how she describes any food that resembles a curry. I have spent the afternoon at the Hamburger Bahnhof. It is comforting to see Stefan's pictures and installations laid out so grandly. It makes me feel close to him. Other than the absence of his voice, I do not find so very much has changed between us since his death. His work transcends the need for contact. It continues to communicate meaning to me.

I came back from the Hauptbahnhof on the circle train to Ostkreuz. My two worst stations for anxiety. I was able to forestall my sense of fear as I walked towards the escalator leading to the platform at the Hauptbahnhof by looking at the ground and concentrating my mind on what I had just seen in the museum. Even so I was clinging to my bag as if the things inside it were about to fall out and be lost. I am pleased with how I have managed my anxiety today. It was a little test, and I think, I passed with a middling grade. I do not want my anxiety to prevent me from seeing Stefan's work. It is so splendid, divine and beautiful as was he.

I deliberately came back to Ostkreuz. It was less about testing my anxiety levels, although that was useful. It was more for the walk back to Andrea's via Rosa Luxembourg. There are a series of pretty streets, ordinary houses that have survived, and that is a rare thing. I especially enjoy them at this time of year. The days are so short that it is already dark, or getting dark, by four. The windows from the houses shed light on to the street making them glow with an orange tone. The curtains not yet closed, I can look into the little basements and ground floors of the houses and catch people in their daily occupations; someone cleaning the carpet, having some tea, a child writing at a desk. I think people keep the curtains open after it is already getting dark, because they wish to prolong the day, because once they are closed, the outside world is blocked out, the day is over, and there is only the night time to look forward to.

The separation from Neil and Noah ought to have been painful. It was so sudden, total and immediate—like a precise incision in the flesh—that I felt little. It had to happen. I regret the disgraceful way I behaved towards Noah. Even that, however, may have been for the best in the long run. It was for me. As I drove from the house that day, thrown out by Neil at Noah's insistence, and having collected a small suitcase of belongings, I was sure I would never return, and I didn't. As it was the vacation, I was able to get a room at my university temporarily before I made my way to Berlin, was startled by Stefan's creative event and made him and the city my new home.

Walking also allows me to reflect. The pictures of domesticity that line the street endorse my hollow reality, prompted by Noah's email about Neil. It prompts a bundle of unexpected feelings. Coinciding with my attempt to narrate my own life, to remember and to explain, these feelings are like the soup I have made for Andrea's dinner. Comforting and piquant, the illnesses of Neil and of myself suggest the lives we might and some say should have led. We, he would have said, meaning he, were so blessed to find Noah at all—a chance fostering unimpeded by over bureaucratic officialdom from a time we can barely now believe in. Everything was in place for our quiet lives to succeed, and I broke it. Or, I am being Neil now, strengthened it into the insoluble bond between them that is now being smashed by a disease none of us understands.

I can imagine Noah, although I still think of him aged 15 or 16 not 30 something, trying to win the argument with the doctors, with the world, over the need to name, diagnosis and treat whatever is ailing Neil. Noah trying and failing, which is for him the worst experience. He knows I failed. I did not fail. I failed to allow the sentimentality that hovers in the shadows to take hold, to create the illusion of our happy lives. I was not happy. It was Noah and Neil's fault. It was fine for me to end it, even if disgracefully. But, and I will say but, the ending was decisive and irreversible. It left no one in any doubt. That was why I did it.

In the email, Noah remembers our summer in Provence. He says it is the happiest memory of his childhood, the happiest summer of his life. He does not point the finger. I hear in his frank words the same tremor of disbelief that Neil must die, and I left for ever and no more summer holidays in Provence.

The fabrication of emotion that I describe as sentimentality is at the heart of my second book, the successor to *Make-Believe*. I wrote *The Illusion of Government* so quickly in the excitement of my new Berlin life and my liberation from the delusion I had spent the five fallow years manufacturing for myself.

Chapter Seven
The Illusion of Government

Now it is time to return to my academic life—briefly—from the events I have been describing. How a book features as an event in a life has been for me to connect the different aspects of who I think I am. Nobody who reads *The Illusion of Government* would believe that its roots were in an escape from a dead end role as wife and mother; a role I had fallen into as a trap unseen. Yet they might believe, but I was not then bold enough to make this assertion directly, that the themes of the book were drawn less from an academic background than the lived life of my emotions. For the illusion of government, the shared societal belief that there is a power of government, a group, or party; individuals and leaders; an establishment or system appears fundamental to the sense of who we are. Yet, the illusion is shattered by every political event and upheaval; war; disaster natural or human made, and we curse those we believe responsible. Even in our so-called democracies, we eschew personal responsibility for the failure of a system be it a traffic accident or epidemic or financial disaster. That is government's nature as an illusion. We believe doggedly despite repeated instances when the illusion proves itself greater than any pretence at prescience or foresight on our behalf by those elected, nominated, designated or self-appointed to wield power and control over us.

This illusion is so bolstered by our systems of political thought, reinforced by the monotonous tomes of political scientists that we take as read the division of powers and all that stuff taught to those who work in, manipulate, commentate on and benefit from government. The illusion is just one—an important one let us say—of the illusions of our contemporary society as it looks unerringly and wearilessly for purpose to combat its failing sense of solidity. We must all bolster up the national and global institutions that have somehow come to be created to represent the achievement of human progress. So science is the great arbiter of truth and knowledge. The connection for me, the journey from *Make-Believe* to *Illusion* was the realisation that science, in its endeavour to control and predict our world, would only ever be deployed by those who created beliefs; and that the greatest and most delusional of those believe is government itself. That government can create the conditions for make-believe; whereas make-believe pursues its own delusional course unabated.

I think that covers it as best I can in a short exposition. For the full arguments, and believe me they are backed by a powerful and apt critique of the political traditions written and enacted of certainly the west. In the controversy that followed, so apposite to the worlds of the publishers and the academics, what was missed was the second theme of the piece. This for me is all the more important, because it was where Stefan helped me most and where, later, I think I enabled his creative brilliance to leave an even brighter contribution.

The power of illusion applied to government, taken in its widest sense, as the systems of power and control exercised by an elite over a society is unassailable, because it is a necessary condition for the project of society. It is the price of society. Yet the cost is high. The cost is the abolition, the wiping out of all other possible illusions. Practically, this is borne out by the way utopias are routinely attacked and banished as the biggest single threat to the project of society through illusion. We cannot imagine alternatives because to do so is to deny our fallen nature (woman's fault, lest we forget). How quick we are to adopt as and when essential the cover of religion and tradition to support the way things are. What is worse, the terror of revolution or the illusion of government? It is clear that we have decided in our make-believe world that illusion trumps all alternatives. How far have we truly travelled from the feudal relationships of our ancestors; courtly love is a happy delusion to fall into, the political equivalent of the illusion of science.

Still we are constantly lured by the baubles of illusion; technology, limitless energy and food, living forever and above all freedom. I feel enabled to inject a degree of emotion, an element of the irrational, into my memoir. It is about my life. To pretend that the insights I wish to share is other than a passionate endeavour would be wrong. I am writing this to protest my guilt of feelings, of sentiment, of a life that trespasses into this weaverbird like rational chamber sealed from the blasts and tempests of human life. That was what nearly finished me off in the fallow years. I very nearly surrendered to the illusion of family life. That was the illusion that Stefan unveiled and that made it possible for me to escape to Berlin and write my second major work.

The Illusion of Government was published in 1997, a year after I had moved to Berlin and abandoned Neil and Noah. It was instantly controversial and successful. It also prompted my return to London to work with the then newly elected Labour Government.

Yesterday, Andrea and I had a beautiful evening. Despite the now very cold weather, we have eaten a simple salad with some grains and a gently sour sweet dressing. Andrea is as always respectful of my limited appetite. She offered and I accepted her kind offer to prepare our meal last night. In the morning, now she is gone, I can reflect on another delightful conversation. She asks me about my work. I continue to speak about my next work, *Providence, Not Progress*, in which I know she is genuinely interested. It is odd that I am writing in a kind of secrecy—a secrecy because no one other than I knows I am doing it—my memoir. I wonder what if anything will become of it. Despite this discrepancy between the book I am actually writing and the book I talk about writing, they are not perhaps so distinct. Andrea, I am sure, suspects something. She probably suspects that my current writing project will be much more personal, much less restrained by academic conventions than my previous three major works. She is genuinely supportive. I spoke to her again about the ideas in *Illusion* as we were eating last night, and she agreed that it was built on the foundation of my lived emotional experience as much and probably more than an academic discourse. She was clear, as I am, that that was the reason for its impact and success, just as the third book, *The Death of the Firm*, written after my experience of advising government had failed to grab anything like the same level of attention.

Andrea invited me to a concert at her university. It was two or three nights ago. I realised, when we attended, that the term was nearing its end. The students and teachers were preparing for Christmas. There were decorations and a sense of excitement. It was familiar but also alien. I was looking forward to the concert. The university hosted a prestigious young string quartet that had won a number of international prizes. The concert was an acknowledgement of the important role the university had played in nurturing the group and was a way of saying thank you and reflecting the traditions of musicianship in the institution. The pieces appealed to me, three Haydn quartets. Each was taken from a different set at separate points in the composer's long life. None, oddly, was known to me. I do know a number of his quartets but he wrote so many, there always remain more. The loveliest movement was the largo from the Opus 15 number one quartet. It was played first, as the pieces were played in the order in which they had been written. Reading the programme note, I tried to remember properly what largo meant. I thought flowingly. Now I have looked it up, and it means very slowly and stately or with dignity. Yet, flowingly was how I experienced the music.

The quartet is a mixture of nationalities and two women and two men. I always wonder how they are able to combine to create this experience for their audience. How immersed are they in the emotional ebb and flux of the musical forms or is it just a job for them where professionalism predominates? I would like to ask them but expect that separating out strands like emotional empathy and professional musicianship would be unhelpful in analysing why this quartet is successful and others are not.

Last night we discussed the concert. I was enthusiastic, and Andrea was pleased that I had enjoyed the event. Now it is very cold, and I am not really enjoying being outside so much. I commented to Andrea that the concert was very seasonal. I was pleased to be involved in the university sharing its success with the quartet at this enjoyable time of year. Andrea was intrigued. She did not think of me as someone who would particularly value Christmas. In the flat, there are a number of small but beautiful decorations so we are not completely pagan. We started swapping stories of our own Christmas traditions. We each had our own horror stories of overly sickly sweet puddings and family rituals that now seem poignant.

Sweetness and sentiment are the attractions of Christmas. This is an undeniable reality. We enact it socially, in families and in our individual fantasies of giving and receiving. I think Andrea's surprise that I would indulge in such sentimentality echoes her knowledge of me. Remember, that dates from my arrival in Berlin in 1995, estranged by my own bad actions from my family and about to embark on a book that discredited the illusion that I had previously embraced in *Make-Believe*. She had not seen this part of me that could and has embraced a perfectly ordinary sense of family.

The largo hums in my heart. It strengthens me against the cold. The winter is making me feel sicker. It does become harder as you get older to endure north European winters. If I could, I would travel somewhere warmer. If I had known Noah from his birth, even from the time before he became a young boy, would I have felt differently? Family life was an illusion for me. An illusion that tried to trap and defeat me. I broke out. Yet, the largo in my heart, I hear it. Would Christmas have been different with a baby, with a small child—my very own Jesus child? Does that create an unforgettable melody?

Noah is sending me emails two or three times a week. They provide carefully edited descriptions of Neil's condition. Edited to exclude his own feelings. These I must imagine or infer, but there is little to go on. He ends the emails affectionately. He hopes I will have an enjoyable Christmas with my German friends. I wonder if he has read any of my books. It is not something I have thought about before. I wonder what he would make of them. I know he won't have read them. His reasoning is sound. If they are good, he will be hurt that I abandoned him; likewise if they are bad.

In 1997, I was appointed as a special advisor to the Minister for Enterprise in the new Labour Government elected by a landslide. It seemed I could not put a foot wrong. Stefan congratulated me. He gave me a scribble, a large bird not completely sketched. The bird might have been a bird of prey or some extinct, useless creature from pre-history. He wrote on the sketch 'Macht oder Gewalt'. He should have known. My excitement as I felt myself led into the corridors of power was tempered slightly as the offices were not in Whitehall itself, but round in Victoria Street. The young woman from the Permanent Secretary's office sent to meet me was courteous and helpful. First she showed me to the Spads' (as we were universally known) office. Helpfully, she pointed out, this was adjacent to the Minister's office which we were allowed to look into as he was not there. Location and power were one thing. Size of office quite another. The Minister's office was large, with an imposingly sized mahogany desk and a sofa and armchairs around a coffee table. The view was straight down Victoria Street towards Parliament Square. There were art works by recognisable artists on the wall. By contrast, the Spads' office (there were to be two of us) was a broom cupboard. It was referred to, I learnt later, by civil servants as the broom cupboard. I think it might actually have been one once. There were two upright chairs and a kind of folding table you might use for a picnic. There wasn't room for anything else.

My helpful guide then showed me around the rest of the building which was largely empty as it was a Friday. I think a deliberate ploy on the part of the civil servants to have a look at me in private without political interference. The Secretary of State's office was more imposing still than his junior ministers. We visited the various floors, and it was explained what each section and branch did. We finished in the minister's private office where I was left with another young woman who told me she was my link person—whatever I needed.

Left with my new link person, I felt a little awkward, but she, clearly an accomplished civil servant already destined for a senior role, set to putting me at my ease by her enthusiasm in meeting what she described as one of the heroines of her university studies. She was able with ease to run through a rapid positive critique of my writing, including *Illusion*, and more impressively, some of my recent scholarly articles on the relationships between global commerce and the power of national governments. I thanked her for her warm and generous welcome. This was power.

I expected to meet Mary in the department, but when she walked in, ignoring my link person and shook my hand by way of welcome, I was still taken aback. My time in Berlin had taken me out of circulation. The arrogant confidence of self-importance that I too had formerly adopted, deserted me. Stefan's congratulatory sketch no longer seemed witty but inane and childish. I touched the quality of power to disable by retaining potency and threat within a charmed circle whose admission was by invitation only. For those in power, Stefan did not exist and momentarily, shaking Mary's hand, I felt neither did I. I was also taken aback by Mary's rudeness to the people in the minister's office. She ordered tea generally to the air to be delivered to the minister's office where we would be meeting. I followed her out of the office ineffectually waving at my link person. Would I be written up as weak and needy? I felt so and that was unexpected.

I knew everything was a test and that failing was impossible to avoid. How you failed, in the eyes of the officials, the advisors, the politicians themselves, that was how you were judged by each group individually, and a shared but unspoken agreement reached about how you may be used. That was decided quickly, probably already in my case. It would never be articulated. There was a rule, I believe, of never commenting directly on issues or personalities. This undisclosed procedure was confounded by the constant stream of official notes of all kinds describing every event, meeting, telephone conversation and probably thought of the minister. A constant running written incontrovertible record of the official as an endless denial of what was known but not said. Knowing what was real was the trick I would need to learn.

Mary was her confident self. I had not seen her for some years. Although, before going to Berlin, the firm had continued to channel money my way through grants and lecture invitations, Mary had not re-appeared. EIAI had thrived, she told me, so much so that it had set itself up as a private sector company, advising governments and businesses internationally. It was seen as a perfect example of how government initiatives could be transformed into private sector engines for economic growth and development. At the point of transfer into the private sector, Mary explained, she had handed over the reins and joined the firm where she now worked. I asked myself what had happened to her moral dilemmas. Undoubtedly, they were now satisfactorily resolved. Could it be so easy, and I knew I had been sold a lie in Rome all those years ago. It had been so convincing, yet I had no idea to what end.

The wooden door with the heavy brass handle was opened, and I suppose, I expected tea, but instead Colin, the minister, entered. Recently made a peer so that he could join the new government, Colin did appear older than when I last saw him. He was followed into the room by my link person who sat quietly noting everything that was said. Colin was effusive in his congratulations to me on my appointment as his Spad—the appointment he had made. I reciprocated with my congratulations on his elevation to a ministerial role. The link person wrote it all down. Then he went over to Mary and kissed her. I think his words were, "Isn't it wonderful, a husband and wife team in Whitehall?"

I knew, of course, that he had divorced his wife. I was very grown up about that. I could hardly complain at his decision, after my convenient departure, to ditch the wife he claimed he must stand by morally or else see his reputation crumble. I had, after all, married Neil, so could not argue that he should have married me. Symmetry was the word he used as an excuse. I also recalled his amusement when he told me Mary had made a pass at him. Things had moved on. I knew that he had married Mary. I knew it in the sense that it was a fact I had been told about, I think in some sort of weird update from the firm, as if it were the announcement of two companies merging. I did not know it in the way it was brashly presented by the warmth of a kiss and embrace between two powerful and disdainful people at the heart of government. Why did it matter more that the link person was there? When everything has to be acknowledged and officially recorded, the only way you cannot pretend that this is corrupt is to make it the most normal thing in the world so that it is accepted and it becomes impossible to question. Where, I asked, was the symmetry in that. It was a symmetry of corruption.

I was thinking a lot. So much time in government is spent thinking things that must never be said and that you cannot acknowledge even thinking. Yet unless you have thought them, accepted them and moved on, you cannot take part. This is why it feels that everything happens so quickly when you are close to power; why decisions that are presented as rational are in fact a weighted calculation on the fly that everyone knows could unravel in seconds. The link person—I am sorry, I simply do not remember her name there were so many—stopped writing. Shall

I pour some tea? I had not noticed the tea arriving. There was too much going on in the room. The minister (Colin!) nodded. The tea was in the bone china tea ware that reminded me of the firm. It was all an extension of the same place. It was the same place. We drank tea, and I spoke about Berlin, the liberation it had provided me academically and how this led to *The Illusion of Government*. Mary laughed at that. They loved it, they explained. They needed new thinking. Now was the opportunity for serious changes in direction for policy for the country. The possibilities were enormous and I would be instrumental in realising them. Colin stood, so we all stood. He gripped my hand and looked me straight in the eye. The meeting was at an end.

I left the room. I left Colin, Mary and the link person. Stood in the corridor outside, I was breathless. My body felt drained of energy, exhausted from having run a marathon. I was slightly dizzy and unsure of my whereabouts. I remembered the Spads room and found the right door. Turning the handle, I made for a chair and sat down. The other chair was occupied. It was the other Spad. We sat like potential dates, our knees nearly touching in the narrow space. He had a laptop open on the folding picnic table and was working at something. We introduced each other. He immediately congratulated me on the success of *The Illusion of Government* confiding that his brief was media so he had in fact only read a summary circulated earlier in the week to all members of the department as part of the briefing on me. I thanked him, being the one person who had not received the briefing on me, but then I knew, I thought, about me. He said my email account would already be set up using a different name from my own, "You know to deal with the media and other riff-raff." He gave me a rapid run down on the kind of media scrutiny I could become subject to if I was interesting. No surprises and no embarrassment were the next two lessons I learnt. I thanked him and wished I had been sent a briefing about him so I could compliment him as seemed the way of doing things. Perhaps I had been sent a briefing to my new email account in a name I did not know. He turned back to his work. He was a busy man, it was clear.

I was not. I had not expected to see Colin, who was not supposed to be in the department on a Friday. Later, I realised, he didn't have a constituency to look after as he was a minister in the Lords. He followed a different routine to many there. The civil servants maintained their chaperoning duties, but he largely relied on Mary and, presumably the firm, for much of the actual policy work in which he was engaged.

Writing this now, it remains unbelievable. I can recall with accuracy that afternoon in Victoria Street. I can recall it as the person woefully naïve as to how power practically works. A person who had made her life a study of the nature of politics and public policy brought up short by a brief experience of the real thing. I can recall myself as the person sat in those meetings trying to keep up with the amount of information I needed to assess and understand. I can recall it as the more chastened academic who felt, after the experience of being a Spad, a need to rethink but not abandon the insights of an earlier version of herself. The question I faced then, my recalled self-faced was whether to continue, whether to wade in more deeply to the practical reality of what I now could see opening before me. I think the answer to this question was not in doubt. Perhaps it is the rationalisation of the chastened academic who argues that I stayed, because this was the unique opportunity given to me to undertake my greatest piece of fieldwork. It would be untrue and unrealistic to believe myself capable of reaching such a conclusion as if, chased by a wild beast, you believed this a perfect opportunity to examine physiological reactions to danger. It was genuine lived experience that brought into question everything that had gone before. So I stayed, I held my nerve, I learnt first-hand the ways of practical government.

The author of *The Illusion of Government* was about to see in direct focus how illusory government really is. Each year, as Christmas approaches, the absurdity of the biblical account of these events veers into more vivid colours of madness. This year in the Berlin winter is no exception. Unusually for us, Andrea and I have gone out for a meal. We are able to avoid the crowds in the Christmas markets, many people sitting outside drinking beer. We venture indoors in a small eatery serving some kind of Asian style food behind Eberswalder Strasse. It is a pleasant walk from Andrea's flat. She has sought it out on a friend's advice that it prepares excellent vegetarian food. I have some noodles and am assured that the soup they come in is really vegetarian. I am confident enough in this part of Berlin to accept the assurance. We drink a small glass of wine each. We join in. It is pleasant. We laugh over some matter or other. I remember us laughing but not about what. It made a pleasant change, we agree. We have now been to the string quartet at the university and for our quiet meal. It is an enjoyable extension to each day and these are happy, festive alternatives to our usual routine.

Now, the day after our outing, my sense of the impossibility to relate the power of religion to the stories of Christmas is more vivid. It troubles me and will not let me be. I hope as the festive season passes it will also wane in its distraction. How can I continue to write this memoir when I fail so completely to understand in any way the impossible logic of religious festivals?

As a special advisor to Colin in his newly created ministerial role, I was obliged to attend specially created courses to learn about the job I had taken on. I was eager to find out this practical side to politics. As an academic and consultant, I remained an outsider to the workings of policy as understood within Whitehall. I quickly learnt that this was true of Colin, despite his networks. The department represented a world that ran on its own terms alongside the firm and the politics of parties and democracy.

We were sent in groups of five to undertake our course. It meant spending three days in a stylish hotel in the country. We were actively discouraged from doing other work or communicating too much with family or friends. For me, this was not difficult. Stefan was largely aloof from the internet. Unless you were physically present, he paid you no attention and rarely then. With me, I know, that was different, but it was my presence not my absence that sustained (I hope!) his artistic flow.

More importantly and rather excitingly, the main academic contribution—alongside talks by senior civil servants and experts in various branches of law and international affairs—was to be by my very own Graham. While I had been making my own success, Graham had clearly been diligent in his pursuit of academic glory. Still at the same university, he was now professor and headed a department he had created himself on the back of his specialism in memorial as history. I won't waste too much time with the intricacies of his theoretical approach. Enough to say that his version of how we remember individuals in the present—artefacts like war memorials and halls of fame—

provide unique insights into how we construct historical narratives.

He explained this to me when we met at the evening reception preceding the course proper. I was pleased he made a beeline for me. We were both excited I recall at the chance to catch up thrown into our paths fortuitously. His daughter was just changing school. I reminded him his wife had been expecting when we last met. He now had a second daughter. Two was good, he explained. He had kept up with my work and had already read *The Illusion of Government* which he was intending to refer to in his teaching session the next day. I suppose it would not really be possible for him to teach us if he had not read my work. More embarrassingly, I had failed to follow his work. He was quick to excuse as he admitted it was a real niche area.

What I had not expected and least of all from Graham was the first slide in his talk. There it was, a picture of Stefan's *Individualisation*. I wish I could see Graham's talk on YouTube, but of course, it was all confidential and to do with government. That was more about deniability than any fear of revealing secrets. Graham did reveal a secret. His address fell on deaf ears. The other four Spads were clearly not engaged by his admittedly convoluted theoretical arguments. They wanted to spend time with the policy theorists. What was extremely popular at that time was the idea of 'voice' and 'choice'. It was all very Blairite, a watered down socialism marching to the rhythm of capitalism. Apparently, as Spads, we owed our loyalty to the politics of the government. The politics of the government meant that voice and choice were needed to justify policy direction. There was no truck with ideas of rights or political ideals. The ideology was that unless people chose what they said they wanted, then it wouldn't happen and resources would be prioritised elsewhere. Our role was to advise on how to create tests that assessed both choice and voice. The theme music was *Wouldn't It Be Nice*.

This was all so much embarrassing guff. The other four were keen to lap it up. I just wanted to absent myself. Clearly, that was impossible in a group of five. On top of which we had our party minders. Their main role was to check in with how we were finding the programme, welcoming feedback as a way of assessing our suitability and progress in embracing the party line. They were also on hand to provide guidance in how to deal with the media (that was not our job, so don't) and censor our public statements and writing. It was all great.

Graham, on the other hand, captivated me. First, I must have been smart to have picked him out at school. He would never be an academic superstar but he had a genuine and personally distinct conceptual style. I enjoyed it and appreciated the small but important insights this provided. Unlike Graham, I would never be able to spend hours reviewing the Guinness Book of Records year by year to identify strong narrative threads relating the history of the present to that of past eras by comparing contemporaneous history textbooks and teaching notes or exam questions and marking schemes. I really did appreciate someone who did do this and left the bigger ideas to people like me. I also discovered that I still liked Graham and believed he liked me despite my, at that time, enormous sense of personal worth and achievement.

Chapter Eight
In Government

Religions are successful, because they show their truths through stories. Only I have never believed in the stories told by religion. Now, Christmas over, I am all the more at a loss how anyone can possibly believe all that stuff. Did anyone ever believe it? I do not know. All the same, it illustrates the difficulty I face each time I sit down to right my memoir. I am more interested in ideas than I am in stories. Yet I have opted to tell my story, my history and I think it is of interest.

If religion needs stories, governments need them more. Against a head wind of bad stories, it wishes to tell the story of achievement, wisdom and kindness for the nation and the world. Graham did not teach us that. He taught us that policy is contingent upon events but must appear ideologically consistent and able to predict and control the future. The true role of the specialist adviser—the Bads as the civil servants mockingly derided us—is to broker that thin defence between events and its arch enemy ideology. Our best friend is to embrace certainty even as the ship is going down, up or along or anywhere but we do not know.

Graham had never met Colin. It occurred to me that Graham would have been better equipped to be his Spad. My general sense was that my appointment was mainly window dressing. I invited Graham to the department and asked Mary whether she would like to meet one of my academic colleagues. She looked askance, did I really think she had any interest in ideas unrelated to power. Well, let us see.

Graham was waiting in the lobby holding his visitor's pass. He had acknowledged how rare it was for him to be in London, let alone in a government department. This struck me as odd since he had been selected to give the course to the Spads.

Perhaps not. Perhaps the other Spads needed topping up on the theory rather than the reality, unlike myself. He stood up to greet me as I came through the barrier. He embraced me, gently, and we exchanged kisses on the cheek as has come to be the fashion. Notwithstanding the generality of the greeting, I felt a gentle kindness in the strength of the embrace. It acknowledged with gratitude a different time. It warmed me in that cold place.

I had borrowed Colin's grand ministerial office for our meeting. Why not use the artefacts of power if you can. There were no civil servants present as this was a private meeting. It meant a little piece of freedom. Mary was already in the office when I ushered Graham into the room. He made some commonplace remarks on its size and elegance. It is difficult not to be mesmerized to some extent by the nature of government. Mary stood and greeted Graham, offering him coffee or tea from the flasks delivered for unimportant meetings. He took his coffee with milk in the too small standard issue bone china teacup and saucer. Mary retook her seat on the sofa, I sat on the armchair and Graham sat on the other sofa facing us both.

I cannot quite at this distance of time remember the conversation verbatim. I am sure, Mary would have started it as a meeting—she had no alternative approach to people or social situations. She would have asked us something along the lines of what was the purpose of the meeting, or what did we or Graham wish to achieve by the end of our discussion. What I do clearly remember is Graham bursting out laughing after Mary's initial enquiry. He snorted with laughter and looked at me in disbelief. Mary, who was never disconcerted, looked at me and then Graham. She sensed it was some joke between the two of us. I sought to reassure her in returning her gaze that I was as uninformed as she was.

Then Graham started talking. He made no attempt to explain his merriment and continued to speak in a merry way, as if he were telling us the most amusing story punctuated by one-liners. He told us our jobs. He took us through how the individual has become fundamental to the strength of capital through their role as a consumer. That in politics, we must necessarily relate to the individual as a consumer. In terms of policy, this meant providing the consumer with choice and voice; that the consumer needs to believe that they are in control and consequences are the result of their decisions and their feedback.

Mary actually listened. She went to the minster's desk to fetch a pad and a pen—all she could find were post it notes—and started to jot down what Graham was saying. I had not seen her do this before. She was clearly engaged, and I spent the time wondering why this was all so funny for Graham. Graham had made his niche academic speciality as a historian by seeing history through the eyes of individuals, beginning with lists of names on US civil war memorials in Manchester-on-Sea, Massachusetts.

I remember standing up. Mary and I both seemed restless, attentive but fidgety. I took Graham's cup and refilled it. I fetched Mary her customary camomile tea with the hot water from the other flask. I opened a packet of biscuits, one of those tiny packs with two pieces of shortbread in cellophane with a tartan edging. Graham was continuing to expand his theoretical approach to policymaking and advice. He did not, as I would have done, followed the route of exploring the delusion at the heart of voice and choice, although he did acknowledge my contribution to the topic. Unique insights, he called them, as he referenced both *Make-Believe* and *Illusion*. Mary failed to pick up the professional slight intended and received by me. It is always the same. I am always seen as this hybrid; neither academic nor politician. Not even a pundit. Well, this book is my answer.

Instead, Graham moved to a different tack, challenging the notion of late capitalism and suggesting we were at the beginning of capitalism, not its end. Labour was a temporary detour. He paused and laughing explained he did not mean that as pun. Mary, momentarily and unaccustomingly blank, he explained he meant labour as in Marx etc. not the Labour Party. The major strength of capitalism was its ability to reinvent labour, for example as the consumer of its own product to generate wealth for the owners.

As I sat down with my unopened packet of shortbread, Mary asked him about voice. She understood what he was saying about choice and consumers, but what about voice. I opened the biscuits and offered them to Mary and Graham who each took one, meaning I needed to get up again to fetch another packet.

From behind me, I heard Graham explaining that voice was about memorialising, about telling stories. That is why the war memorials were so important. Voice overtook great people as capitalism required people freely to surrender power. Voice was coercion disguised as volunteering. The volunteers die, and they are memorialised. Now we are even better at this. We make awards, run TV shows, create celebrity. It is the golden truth that we are nowadays each a celebrity at the centre of our lives. Every day we watch ourselves on TV, star in our favourite role. Graham was laughing out loud. Voice and choice, yet he never denied it; never let on, except in his casual acknowledgement of my work, that is was all made up.

I remained standing by the table with the refreshments, not turned towards Mary listening to Graham. As I stood, I fiddled with the second packet of biscuits. Graham continued to guffaw as he spoke. Mary continued to write on the post it notes, using them as a makeshift and clumsy notebook, turning each one over when she had written on it instead of pulling them off.

Simultaneously, the idea for *Death of the Firm* in the form of its title took hold in my head as I failed to notice its inherent failure as a strong enough idea. That would only become painfully apparent later after its publication, Foreword by Lord Colin himself!

After saying goodbye to Graham in the department's lobby, I returned to Colin's office for a brief follow up with Mary. "Such an interesting man," she said. "It is fun to have all these ideas, quite another thing to be in power."

I knew then it was inevitable Graham must meet Stefan. I must be the broker. It needed it to go well. I would remain, out of politeness, as Colin's Spad for two years while I wrote *Death of the Firm* and then find the time to regret both being a Spad and writing that bad book. The firm, the one Mary still worked for, was not the same as the firms I described as dying in the global economy of fungible government. In my heart, and I can admit this here, it was that firm I wanted to kill off in writing such a treatise. Its complete immunity to any such threat consigned that work to failure. It was not ridiculed. It was politely reviewed and subsequently ignored. I know I wrote it in too much of a hurry and with too much confidence. When you have learnt to come and go as you please in a government department, with civil servants obliged to treat you with apparent respect and respond reasonably to your requests, then you become too sure of yourself. It is the same confidence that makes all governments, all regimes vulnerable in the end to overreaching. I fell into that trap, although I only spent two years with Colin. I left of my own free will, explaining to Colin in one of the rare opportunities I was given to speak to him, that I could only play such a role for a short period. I needed distance. In fact, the Spad role was more an opportunity for me to experience government, to reference my work from an internal view of how it all worked. That experience needed not to overtake my academic stance. That stance was itself most criticised for the subjectivity of its frame of reference. I never tired of explaining that the subjectivity was the whole point.

Once I had left the role, at the end of 1999, the year of Stefan's 50th birthday, I published *Death of the Firm* written in less than 12 months while working as a Spad. I knew that after I left, Mary would announce she had sacked me. It became more and more apparent during those first two years of the then new Labour Government, that Colin was increasing his political clout, and with it the clout of the firm. For those of us who associated the firm with the misery and oppression of Thatcher and her successors, there was no small leap to re-imagine it as the expert agency on which new Labour depended for what it called policy implementation. Everyone at the firm brought their unimpeachable equality credentials to the table. Me for Colin. Mary never failing to mention her two years as an aid worker before realising she need to influence at a global level the exercise of power and the allocation of resource. Well, at the firm she certainly did that. I sound bitter because I am.

In Colin's office, after Graham's visit, Mary wanted to continue the discussion with me on our own. I was happy to oblige, explaining that I had known Graham from school, that we had in fact been together for a while at college until we had each gone our separate ways. I took a view, the correct one I think, that honesty was a good policy. I knew, because I was told, that I had been checked out—"vetted"—so did not wish to be seen as having anything to hide. Yet Mary's line of questioning was not satisfied. She wanted to know how I felt about him when our paths crossed at the Spads' course. I had been delighted and rather taken aback. I did not know what Mary wanted from me, from this now interrogation, so I asked her.

She was, unlike myself, reticent. So I took the initiative and asked her if she minded about me and Colin—our history. She looked at me blankly. I stumbled and said something along the lines of, "He must have told you." Clearly, he had not. She didn't follow the course of the discussion, abruptly changing it to ask me why Graham had been so comical. I did not know then, and I still have no idea. Maybe he found the whole idea of him being of use to government slightly absurd; as if he had been asked to perform in a ballet or take a part in Puccini's Madame Butterfly.

Graham contacted me a month later through the department email address I was using and he had from my attendance at his course. He wanted to meet. He wanted to check out a couple of things. He wrote he preferred to do this in person and not at the department. That suited me. I was already beginning to suffocate there. Mary treated me respectfully but distantly. The civil servants read the situation precisely and mirrored her behaviour. I didn't mind. I continued to enjoy unrestricted access to all discussions and documents and do not think there was any conspiracy; just a pecking order. I hardly saw Colin at all. Was Mary jealous? This seemed very hard to believe. It was quite difficult to see Mary and Colin as a couple in any other sense than business partners. That was their affair.

We met at the Friends Meeting House café opposite Euston Station. Graham said he was on the way back to his university after a meeting in London. I wasn't sure he hadn't made the journey just to speak to me. He was uncomfortable with what he wanted to say to me. First, he asked me how I enjoyed the Spad role. As usual, I was honest. I enjoyed the access and the closeness to power. It wasn't for the long term. Practical politics belonged to the Colins and Marys of the world. I was ruthless in my own way. It would provide unique material for my next book. I had the title and was arranging in my head the arguments, the ideas and the chapter headings.

My openness relaxed him. He had been asked to move away from the Spads courses, a phrase that struck me as peculiar. It meant the same as being let go, he was obliged to tell me. Telling me upset him, and he was open about how upset he had been when this had happened. He attached personal kudos to the role, believed that he was making a real contribution and had earned the respect of his colleagues for this role. There had been nothing unpleasant in how he had been handled, except the effective termination of his contribution.

I tried to reassure him along the lines that it was generally chaos not conspiracy—that at least I could testify to even after a relatively short time. There was probably some new initiative from the Cabinet Office. I was already long enough in the tooth to speak with confidence of the source of the most nutty ideas in Whitehall.

Graham nodded but sadly. He wanted to ask me directly, and did, whether I thought the meeting he had held with me and Mary might have been the cause. That made sense in terms of the timing of his being moved away. He was terribly upset, and I felt bad about having erroneously and foolishly brought him too close to this part of my world. I didn't confirm his suspicion about Mary. It chilled me, because it was at the least of it more than plausible. It chilled me more, because I made a connection between my mistake in disclosing that there had been a past between Colin and me and the possibility that Mary had acted out of spite towards Graham whom she could see was a friend and part of my history.

Everything moved so quickly in those two years of Spadship. My brain had to speed up. By that I mean I acquired the ability to process large amounts of information very quickly. First by filtering out what was noise, and then by making rapid connections to reach conclusions and give advice. I had no way of knowing whether I filtered out the right stuff or made the right connections, but I knew the advice—what to say or not say, where to be or not be, who to speak to or not—was good. As I write in *The Death of the Firm*, one of the principal reasons government outstrips commerce is its skill at managing the news. So it was with the advice Spads and others provide. It may be incorrect, based on an inaccurate reading of the situation, but if you are smart enough, your reading becomes the media reading of the situation. Politicians make their own news agenda, or they are lost. Colin was superb at that branch of power, and I did contribute.

I believed my analysis for Graham's departure sufficiently to apologise to him there and then. I was also sincerely sorry he had been so upset. I didn't explain the detail. I just wanted him to know that knowing me probably hadn't helped. Inviting him to the department—my idea entirely—was a mistake. It was a mistake that had originated from my need to show off. It was naïve, and Graham had been hurt as a result.

As I became increasingly mournful and self-accusatory, Graham cheered up. He offered me his sympathy, not to beat myself up, and thanked me for my honesty. I felt mean and foolishly selfish. Power despises personal neediness. Any chink in an armour of self-invulnerability, any need for endorsement or self-doubt, is ruthlessly eliminated by power's fear of being found out. Graham went to get us both a second cup of coffee. He was laughing again. It was the same mirth he displayed to such poor effect in Colin's office. Now it cheered me up. I felt forgiven, like a child. Graham, I remembered had children. When he brought the second round of coffees, I asked him about them.

Today something has changed. This is not to do with the passage of my life that I am writing about. I don't think so. It has to do with the light. I have taken an unusual walk for me. Down the Karl-Marx-Allee, that wide, trafficy reminder of the East that it has not been possible to erase or soften. There is nothing attractive for the walker here. The breadth of the road is not that of a boulevard but of a dual carriageway. It is featureless, or the features are part of a then futuristic and unrealised vision of utopia. The East made its make-believe, the West invented theirs on TV. On TV superheroes and comic characters thrive. In the made make-believe they are a dystopian reality conjured in the West by the tabloids as child abusers, serial killers and mass rapists. The tabloids, where comic book TV meets reality hand in hand.

The change in the light is not seasonal. Even though we have now entered the trough of winter, hiding in its dull, cold trench of seasonality unapologetic. The light is dimmer, dimmer than the winter light that should at least be bright against the pallor of the sky's shifts from puddle, tarmac grey to sapphire blue. I take the U-Bahn home. The usual anxieties that I am going to fall from the platform or be blown away. I walk deliberately down the centre of the platform, head slightly bowed to avoid seeing the edge of the platform and avoiding my fear of the chasm it represents. The light, the strange choice of route for my walk combine to drive me on to the U Bahn to escape exposure of Karl-Marx-Allee. Normally, it is easier on the U Bahn than the S Bahn. The trains appear more like a model railway. Today, they thunder, and I feel their power and the intransigence of the steel and mechanics that propel them through the city. I fear them, and I fear the dimmer light. I fear it is my eyes. Is the light the same, and it is my eyes that have dimmed unable to absorb the fleeting pictures of the city even as I walk head down to block the wider view?

A woman is looking at me on the platform. I do not catch her eye, but in looking up, she knows that I have seen her—a much younger woman. She looks away with a disdainful half smiled grimace. She feels so securely superior to me, so thankful not to be me. For what it is worth, I feel the same towards her, but would rather feel a sentimental attachment to someone who could have half a heart towards this mad woman walking head down along the dead centre of the platform as if at the edge of a high precipice.

Now, back at the kitchen table, writing this, I have calmed. It is difficult to form an objective measure of such subjective feelings as anxiety catching a train. I think it has got worse. It means a more heightened sense of anxiety. I am worried if I cannot take the U Bahn any longer. I am less worried about not being able to use it as how I shall explain this to Andrea or to other people. You go ahead, I prefer to walk. It is absurd.

I cannot help but contrast Andrea and Mary since I have now brought Mary back to life—what has since happened to her is not known to me. Colin and I lost touch after I left my role as his Special Advisor, and my links with the firm were ended by my abrupt departure. Betrayal and largesse scorned are not forgivable. They simply were no longer in contact. I was politely eliminated from the network. Andrea's is the steady and deliberate career of the true academic—researcher, author, teacher—without distraction. It is an example of what I should have done and never could have done instead of my hybrid of politics, research and writing. But Mary, always she would remind us of her two years of aid work as if that qualified her for something. Two years in a lifetime of brokering, men and women, power and resource, interest and exploitation. In a fairy story, she would have been sent to work in a leper colony for a year and a day, but no fairy story could predict that she would have ended up how and where she did.

I am still not sure what has changed other than the dimmer light. I am now also anxious that I am outstaying my welcome with Andrea. I don't think this is the case. It just troubles me as a thought, as a possibility. As a possibility it reminds me that I have no alternative. I mean I can go back to London and live there. I have somewhere to live in London, but it does not seem like an alternative. I want to speak to Andrea about this when she gets back. Christmas was a distraction from having to think about the future. Maybe that is why I have stopped writing *Providence, Not Progress*, because I only want to look at the past and am too scared of the future. It is too uncertain. The future is not a place I expect to be spending much time. So how do you spend the time between non-diagnosis and the onset and conclusion of the disease? Without a diagnosis, there is no prognosis, no plan, no purpose or direction. I remain writing to fill the gap between two points that are not described, may not exist, the then then and the then now.

Graham and I maintained a regular communication after our encounter at the Spads training session. I took an increasing interest in his work. I had known about it only second hand and now had the opportunity to read his original papers. In our regular correspondence—it was more convenient geographically to email than to meet—I regularly asked him teasingly why there was still no book. He admitted that he much preferred researching—grubbing around as he put it—to putting pen to paper. When he did write, he preferred the discipline of the academic paper to what he saw as the burdensome task of producing a whole book. He wanted to capture ideas crisply and impersonally. He wondered if I might ghost write something for him. I was certainly tempted but turned him down on the grounds that it would be nearly impossible to exclude my personality, my slightly non-academic take in the style of my presentation. He understood. He wanted the anonymity of the paper and shied away from a personal style. There was the ever-present academic frown even in his light heartedness. That has always for me the unavoidable condition of how I am.

I had immediately known when Mary explained Graham was unnecessary that he must meet Stefan. It is difficult to think of two different versions of a person. Graham had with unconscious deliberation adopted the persona of the apologetic and reticent lecturer. He left the slightest impression that he knew stuff that was important and profound—sufficiently slight that you were wary not to buy completely into his demeanour. Stefan enacted alienation.

I will speak to Andrea this evening. Tomorrow, after writing, I will take the S Bahn to the Hauptbahnhof so that I can look again at Stefan's work in the Hamburger Bahnhof.

The emails from Noah have increased in number and become more frequent. He enjoyed Christmas. His own family, I forget he has a wife and children, or even how many, spent the time visiting Neil as Neil appears increasingly housebound. So they transferred their family Christmas to the Tooting house. He describes the problem of having purchased a Christmas tree that was too tall for the living room. I suppose Noah's family home has higher ceilings. They tried to fix it up in the hall, but the children objected that it was not in the living room. Also it made manoeuvring Neil's wheelchair almost impossible. So the solution was to buy a saw and saw off a foot of the trunk and some of the lower branches. He attached an explanatory photo to the email. The children are waving (two, a girl and a boy about 10 and 11). In the background I could see the back of someone—presumably his wife.

I know nothing of Noah or of his family. If asked I would be unable to tell you their names. Yet he now emails as if I am a close friend of the family. Friend, I think, not relative. Definitely not a parent. In that he is right. I have never really been a parent. He wants to be in touch. The conditions are that we forget how we came to know each other. We blank out my putative adoption. Perhaps for the best. It was never legally formalised. I wonder if Neil has somehow formalised his paternity. I'm sure Noah will have put it on some proper footing. He is after all the successful lawyer.

My email replies are briefer. I intend them to be friendly, matching Noah's newfound style of elegant bonhomie. I wonder if I shall see him, if Neil will be alive next Christmas—and me. Families think that every year will be the same. Now Christmas is over Noah's two children will be imagining next Christmas. Transferring everything—presents, food, whatever else they need to grandpa's house in Tooting. Buying a Christmas tree that is too large for the living room. Arguing over whether it can go in the hallway. Sawing off its lower trunk and branches. Reliving the past by imagining the future. Yet, families outgrow their memories faster than we can mount photos in our albums. We think each year there will be the same family holidays, the same Christmases. Just like Provence. We planned to go back every year and never went back once. I have not been back there since.

Last night I spoke with beautiful Andrea. Beautiful because she understands. I have postponed my trip to the Hamburger Bahnhof from this morning until tomorrow. My excuse is that heavy rain is forecast all morning. It is raining really hard outside right now. I explained to Andrea how I am feeling. She reassured me. She told me that not only was I welcome to stay, but she wanted me to stay. She embraced me a little, and we opened a bottle of wine. That is quite rare. It was not a celebration. It was a homecoming event. That is what Stefan would have called it, an event. Without events the world does not exist. There is no homecoming without an event. The wine tranquilised any anxiety I felt yesterday evening. Andrea allays anxiety.

The Noah emails are not a good sign. I worry about Neil, about myself. I must hasten on to explain how I brought Graham and Stefan together; how events conspired to bring them into each other's range of possibilities. Stafan's Voiceless Events.

Chapter Nine
The Absence of Symmetry

Stefan's 50th birthday took place in Berlin near where I am writing now a week or two after the actual date of his birthday. It was in late August 1999 when there were still venues available from the former wall torn Berlin suitable for this old East German renegade made good in the liberal climate of hope that has long since expired. I was still, after two years, working as a Spad with Colin and the Blair Government. After two years, I think only a little of the excitement and sheen of the Labour 1997 landslide had rubbed off. We were all still hopeful. I think that is right. It must have been before the slide into war mongering with the US that marred Blair's reputation so badly and did such long term damage to Labour. Although I continued to work as a Spad, I knew that it could not continue for too much longer. Mary treated me now more or less like a less able member of the civil service. I saw nothing of Colin, and did not regret that. I regretted my lost momentum and already the outline of *Death of the Firm*—that benighted book—was taking shape in my mind. There were no intimations until the Stefan's birthday party of the anxiety and sickness that now haunt me.

Whether correct or not, I invited Graham to Stefan's birthday party. Party is a loose description. Although the excitement and radicalism of Stefan's live events when I had first come to know him was now over and the creative potential exhausted, eventing was not. Stefan's friends, who were hosting the party, had found a large empty industrial space in which they had erected six-foot black and white photos of some of Stefan's most substantial works. They were mounted like billboards, double sided so that you walked through the space looking up and around at images processed from mainly his installations. The party was intended as a surprise that proved impossible to keep. So inviting Graham was not a big deal. It was a mainly open invitation to anyone who wished to attend and was sufficiently au fait.

The absence of chairs means that I am sitting on the floor by myself. Stefan has made a speech comparing his life to a popular café now showing signs of wear and inevitably experiencing declining popularity. There is laughter and applause. Who can believe an artist is in decline when his work is illustrated on six-foot boards across this large empty space. I too think he is not quite correct; that his decline as a worn place of refreshment is something worth attending to for the next few years. We do not know he will die in ten or so years' time. But then, that would not have been important except to accelerate the pace of his work. That is how I would have looked at it.

In describing myself, sitting on the floor, listening to Stefan but unable to see him as he was hidden behind one of the boards, I am in some disbelief that this can have been a real part of my life. It is a recorded event, like a video of oneself, like the video of me presenting to the conference many years before this. These recorded images of my past as I seek to identify and assess turning points. This was a turning point.

If Colin no longer needed me or gave me any heed, Graham was happy to rescue me with his attention and good humour. My invitation had happily coincided with his own involvement in a case in Berlin. He had been invited to comment as an historical expert on controversial plans to put up a plaque on a building in Schöneberg, commemorating three Berlin Jews who had lived there before being murdered in the Holocaust. I found it amusing to hear Graham, the eminent professor, being called in as an expert. The controversy was local to the residents of the street and the block where it was proposed to erect the plaque. One of the residents was a history teacher and a great admirer of Graham's work. She had contacted him and invited him and the residents and their supporters had got together money for his airfare. He was staying with the teacher on her sofa. He brought her to the party too.

Graham and the teacher treated the party like an art exhibition. I partly accompanied them as they walked around the billboards—nowadays they would be photographing them. They were intrigued. Neither knew Stefan's work first hand. Graham had searched the internet for information about Stefan when I invited him to the party, but had not heard of him previously except from me. Stefan was so much part of my understanding of everything that I struggled to comprehend how they could not be aware of his work. Yet this is always possible. The teacher, Ursula, had not read my work. I was momentarily irritated that she knew Graham's work so well and yet had never heard of me! Still this is deeply symptomatic of the fragmentation of knowledge (learning?) as we feel our way through to a conclusion. Here was I trying to produce grand schemes (how I still regret *Death of the Firm*), while Ursula and Graham focused on the surviving memorial of tiny lives, obscure, distant and impossible to construct even as a character in a book.

I should have stopped then and there. Listening to them, to their intelligent responses to just photos of Stefan's work, I should have known that I was overreaching myself. Exactly as I had overreached my authority and influence as a Spad by inviting Graham to meet Mary so now too was I about to overreach the possibility of academic commentary by scrawling *Death of the Firm*. Even to this day I continue to ask, was it really that bad? How bad could it really be? Yet it remains my last completed book, written and published in haste in 2000, ten years before Stefan's death. Now only this memoir and the idea of *Providence, Not Progress*. That book is conceived but not written. Instead I have been diverted on to this side road of my memoir.

Graham and Ursula asked me if I could fix for them to meet Stefan. As that was really why I had invited Graham in the first place, I was keen to oblige. Now, having seen his work, they both wanted to enlist his support in the plaque campaign. They calculated that having such a heavyweight from the arts world in Berlin would swing the campaign totally their way. I was impressed how quickly they moved from complete ignorance of Stefan to brash admiration and acquisition.

I was again taken aback when Stefan told us, when we met for a coffee a few days later, that he knew about the case of the plaque and was profoundly moved by it, or more precisely, by the heart and strength of the campaign to have it put up. Ursula looked thrilled and gratified. Graham was laughing. I felt out of the swim, not able to keep up. Ursula, I could see, was already enchanted by Stefan in the way I recognised I had been—even

Andrea had been very briefly—we all were for a time. Charm as creative genius disguised Stefan's rather ugly, difficult history projected through his mean appearance and terrible clothes. He adopted East Germany as style, his style, and insisted on reminding his public and even more those close to him (whatever that actually meant) that history was unresolved. History, he explained to the history professor and teacher was an attempt to memorialise, a competition. The plaque was a memorial, but a memorial to the voiceless. To be nameless is to be forgotten. To be named is to be labelled.

I have postponed going to the Hamburger Bahnhof. I blame the weather. I know the real reason is that I am too afraid to take the S Bahn, especially at the Hauptbahnhof. Andrea has asked me why I am not doing my usual trips out. I say I am doing the groceries each day. This is true and she does not question me further. She wants to but thinks better of it. Each day is getting harder. I feel truly loved by Andrea and I truly do love her. That is the treasured part of my life.

At Stefan's birthday party, later at the cafe where I introduce him, and by chance Ursula, to Stefan, I see myself as the observer. I am removed from the action. Yet it enables me to watch, and now I am ready to record this part of the changes that have, so to speak, unhinged me.

Graham spoke easily with Stefan. He answered the questions Stefan asked about his academic work. Graham explained the plaque on the London Underground HQ building; how this had stimulated him to explore people named but unknown to history. To explore them as a lens for a historical approach to understanding the relationship between—Graham laughed as he said it—the individual and society. Stefan asked him why he laughed and Graham spoke of not wanting to sound ridiculous. He meant pompous. Stefan was briefly eloquent on growing up in the East, and Graham graciously accepted the thanks Stefan gave him.

'METROPOLITAN DISTRICT RAILWAY COMPANY
THIS STONE WAS LAID ON 24TH SEPTEMBER
1928
BY THOMAS AUTON
HOUSEKEEPER 1899-1929
FOR 43 YEARS A SERVANT OF THE COMPANIES'

Graham's research fell into that long historical tradition of populist re-enactment. What distinguished Graham's approach was the thoroughness of his adherence to available sources. His breakthrough work, on the American civil war based on war memorials naming those killed, had established a reputation for a reliable scholar able to piece together facts in a way that let others draw their more fabulous conclusions. Graham appeared never to resent this.

Ursula was becoming restless with the conversation that excluded her as much as me. She fidgeted with her coffee cup in a way that drew attention to her exclusion. Stefan would never be bothered, but Graham was sensitive to Ursula, especially as she was the principal cause of his visit. He re-introduced Ursula into the conversation and asked more general questions about Berlin before and after the wall came down. What had changed and how much of the change was superficial and how much really changed. Stefan's attention, I could see, veered away from this topic. He was not immune from the German problem of shocked dumbness on the history front. Whether this was the cause or not, Graham laughed. Two historians with an artist, all unable to speak about history unless it was of the London Underground in the early part of the twentieth century.

Graham's ability to humourise matched his skill in never taking sides, never making judgements, never seeking approval or showing concern over his own status vis-à-vis another. I had always known this, but not seen it before so clearly. Probably because before now I had always seen this as a weakness and to my advantage. Now it dawned on me that Graham's advantage, how he made his way was to be unthreateningly useful to other people. Yet this unwillingness or inability to seek power ultimately led to his termination as a contributor to government. What Mary had seen and despised was a man uninterested in power. I am reluctant to acknowledge Graham in this way. I saw it then, because I had become an observer. Although I voluntarily and for reasonable reasons left my post as Colin's Spad, for me it was also a termination, a failure, a moment that marked the decline in my own career, my power, my reputation, my ability to make a personal future that counted in my own terms of reckoning.

Ursula was suggesting a tour of parts of where the wall had stood. Stefan was immediate and vehement in his refusal to take part, in his opinion that any such tourist stunt was an affront, a failure to apprehend, an anti-historical act of vandalism, a denial of his personal artistic vision. It was a strong and stark statement; violent, and I think Stefan might even have stood up as he said it. Graham looked puzzled. I realised Stefan had been speaking to Ursula in German. Graham could clearly see the strength of Stefan's emotions, but did not understand what he was saying. Graham wanted to know if this was about the plaque to the Jewish Holocaust victims. Stefan sat down if he had been standing and was calm. He said he wanted to support the plaque. He told Ursula that Graham had convinced him that such a plaque, the naming of names of unknown people, was an act of importance, an act of justice, an artistic act. Ursula was immediately grateful and delighted and began annoying Stefan even more by overenthusing about his support. That was a hard part of Stefan to accept. It was not enough to excuse his lack of graciousness and manners on the grounds that he was an artist. Even less so that he had grown up in the East. That was a crime then and now to demand special pleading any more than any gratitude or blame was owed the West for how things happened. It was all just history. No one could be held to account because it was unforgiveable but everyone needed redemption, nameless, unremembered, voiceless, forgotten, unheard. The people we all become in Graham's version of the past.

Ursula's plaque was erected a year later after the intervening months of wrangling. Der Tagesspiegel covered the ceremony which was attended by local residents. There was a polite discussions of the merits or otherwise of memorialising the victims in such a way when already there were works underway for the major public Berlin memorials. It was suggested that in future the city authorities should prepare ordinances for further plaques while others argued strongly for the rights of individuals to express their solidarity with victims of the past be upheld. I went to the unveiling ceremony—nothing special. Stefan was in the crowd. I waved, and he nodded but headed off just as it was ending so I was unable to speak with him. Meantime, he had asked Graham to become his historic advisor on his next project, *Voiceless*.

The millennium year was not brilliant for me. No longer Colin's Spad, I had returned to Berlin, to the university post Andrea kept warm for me. I completed *Death of the Firm*. It was either ignored or received poor reviews. The only relief was that bad reviews contrasted it with the brilliance of my earlier work. I still think it has a lot to offer, that the firm as conceived in the first centuries of capitalism had become defunct replaced by global capital in collusion with national governments and the institutions of international relations. That firms, shareholders, the self-employed were all going the same way as labour unable to hold their own in controlling and allocating resources. Nobody was listening. Everyone was hugely confident in the future. I watched this in Germany from Berlin; from Berlin and the East.

Each year I visit the street to check on the plaque. It has not caused neo-Nazi groups to graffiti the walls of the residential block with swastikas as those opposed had argued. It is now weathered and barely distinguishable from the cement wall against which it is mounted. Nothing at all has happened to it. The names are just there, like the name of Thomas Auton. Three Jews who lived in Berlin until they were deported to their murder as the seminal crime, with slavery, of the modern western world. I visit on the anniversary of the unveiling, when I had watched Stefan leave slightly before the end of the ceremonials. The anniversary date is approaching, caught on the cusp of spring. My intention will be to visit this year—I have not missed a year—petrified into Berlin my return visits to London more intermittent and briefer now. Fewer reasons to return there.

2010, the year Stefan died, I was living in London still asking myself whether I belonged there or in Berlin, or in reality was always a visitor in one or the other. Just as since a while I feel I have been always an observer, not free to make my way unimpeded—voiceless. That makes me laugh. Me, voiceless, yet that is a fairly accurate description of how I have been for well over a decade. I have yet to find a publisher willing to take up

Providence, Not Progress. My former publishers have been taken over numerous times and their editors replaced or outsourced or digitalised. It is unavoidable, I understand, but it is also reasonable to be allowed a little maudlin sentimentality for how things once were done. When I belonged to networks of people, not networks. It may be my failure to keep up, a loss of nerve for which I blame Mary's confidence, the way I overreached myself. She let me fail. She never knew about my affair with Colin until I told her, and she had the opportunity for making good on that piece of personal history.

Mary and Colin adopted two children and moved to Hampshire to raise them. Mary became managing partner in the Firm's London office. Colin just carried on doing what Colin always did—being powerful—more powerful now he was a member of the House of Lords and served three successive Labour Governments as minister. Minister for this and that, I think of him. He would be amused that I see myself as a victim of a system I thought I could see right through. How illusory, I could hear him saying, amusing his colleagues and acquaintances. I was absent. I wondered, more maudlin sentimentality, if he thought of me or followed what had become of me. I suspect not.

I missed Stefan's funeral. I excused myself on the grounds that he was now so famous he had become virtually a state function. It was all international dignitaries and political leaders. They said they were celebrating something. I kept away. I was glad to have the excuse. Andrea told me I was wrong and that is why I accepted the invitation to attend the memorial lecture conference. The lectures she edited and failed to persuade me to make a contribution. Graham was one of the speakers. He had continued to work with Stefan on the endlessly unfinished *Voiceless.* Despite being unfinished, there were plans to reveal it in the state in which he had left it at a major posthumous exhibition the following year. That was where I first saw it. Graham's lecture was familiar. It did not take us beyond the anonymity of being named and memorialised to the essence of *Voiceless,* and although it is now a truism to claim it as Stefan's greatest work, it really is true. Irritatingly, it does show the old chestnut of the depth of late style in the unfinished, unfinishable work.

I invited Graham to come with me to see the plaque. Not on this occasion, the anniversary of its unveiling, but subsequent to Stefan's memorial lecture conference. We had had an intermittent email correspondence but not met since 2000. In his older face I saw my own aging. Why these ten years and the years since then until now have passed so undisturbed, unperturbed by ruptures of love or sense of time, I do not know. Graham was telling me on the U Bahn about the notebooks he had kept during the making of *Voiceless*. I found it difficult to hear him. I held my hands up to my ears, and he stopped until we got off the train. Then on the platform, he started again. There were ten notebooks, he said. He was intending to donate them but didn't know where. I suggested the Hamburger Bahnhof which even then had acquired *Individualisation*. I couldn't find the right street, so we ended up walking along several of the adjoining roads. This part of Berlin had been severely bombed. As a result it was a hodgepodge of buildings. Original streets would abruptly terminate in sixties estates showing signs of aging. Even in 2010, Berlin still lacked a sense of civic coherence, or its coherence was its history: distraught, outrageous, flamboyant, perverse. When we finally found the street and the building and the plaque, it was now a poor memorial. Graham was right. Memorials only serve to help us forget individuals and remember events; memorialise history.

Graham had left Berlin by the time *Voiceless* went on display. It was shown in one of the grand banqueting rooms in the Staatliche Kunstsammlungen buildings. In the city where Stefan grew up and lived, where we visited when I knew him best in 1995 and he created *Individualisation*, the work I want to visit again but cannot because of my anxiety. I never read Graham's notebooks, although I have picked up the gist of some of them as they are revered by Stefan's critics who believe they provide vital insights into his work and creativity.

Voiceless is built as an installation. It contains a corridor, similar to a dark and rather unpleasant corridor from one of those sixties blocks of flats Graham and I kept getting lost between when we went to see the plaque. From the corridor, there are three doorways, one to the right, one to the left and one straight ahead. The corridor is narrow, so the number of people able to visit the installation is limited and when I went to see it the corridor was crowded with people pushing past each other to see what is going on. The sense of enclosure is completed by low ceiling and old-fashioned 60-watt bulbs hanging naked from green enamelled round metal shades that serve no obvious purpose.

Each of the rooms has the vestige of an original purpose. Straight ahead is the kitchen. To the left is the bed sitting room. To the right is the bathroom. Only a few articles are left in the rooms. Enough to understand what they were for. The rooms are not quite derelict but also are not quite habitable unless in desperation. It looks like the place a homeless person might live in for a while after somehow stumbling across it and hoping that they would not be found and asked to leave. All the doors, including the door to the corridor where you enter the installation, have been taken off their hinges and lent against the walls. They are painted in neutral, dull colours that have faded so, like the flat, if this is a flat, they have not seen any fresh paint for many years. It always makes me think of generations of people passing without the means or desire to renew their surroundings. Take them as found. Pass through. There is no glimmer of pleasure in these surroundings. I do not know if I am sufficiently communicating how small the corridor and the rooms are. They appear life size and yet for me each time I visited they seemed just slightly too small, but in no way miniature. I am not the only one to have noticed this. Commentators have spoken of Stefan's unique use of visual perspective to achieve this. You stand, jostled, inside an installation that feels like you are in a traditional two-dimensional acrylic painting on the wall. But you are not. You are inside Stefan's own creative genius.

It is not clear in what way the work is unfinished. Stefan refused to show it during his lifetime. He hid it away in a warehouse, working on it there almost every day during the last ten years of his life. He produced many other works during this time. *Voiceless* seemed to be a secret; a part of his work that he refused to let go or anyone to see. That is why Graham's notebooks are seen to be so important. Graham was allowed to visit and see the work. He advised Stefan while Stefan worked on the project. Stefan insisted that Graham remain silent about these conversations. He was not allowed to photograph the work or describe it. Graham did, however, make notes. In his own practical way, he had no hesitation in making these notebooks available publicly as soon as Stefan had died.

I spoke to Andrea about it when we had our now habitual conversation in her sitting room after dinner. I had cooked. Nothing special—pasta with a vegetarian sauce. We both enjoy the simplicity of the dish although it requires a couple of hours of preparation. Simplicity achieved with effort. I still haven't had the courage to tell her the real reason I keep delaying my next visit to see *Individualisation*. Sometimes I wonder if Andrea is able to see Stefan's work beyond her sense of annoyance with him. Annoyance at his masculinity, his egoism, his indifference to politeness, to people and to social etiquette. Andrea is careful not to show this annoyance to me, but I am able to read it in her. The things that annoyed her attracted me, for better or worse. They are all failings (I guess), but of course for me Stefan was and is divine, and gods can make their own rules, especially around social etiquette. My god.

Andrea is very straightforward about the notebooks. She thinks absolutely that Graham did the right thing. I knew this, but I wanted to speak of it, because I am writing about it here, and we tend to spend a bit of time each evening running through what I am writing although Andrea continues to believe that I am writing *Providence, Not Progress*. In a way I am. I am less cut and dried than Andrea. The notebooks perhaps detract from *Voiceless* by appearing to give insights which are nothing more than the conversations and observations between Stefan and Graham. Andrea tells me this sounds more like envy, that I did not have Graham's privileged access. So that is true. Maybe the same criticism I am making of Graham's immediate decision to disclose the notebooks is hypocritical. After all, am I not writing myself about how I think I influenced or was at least a part of the creation of *Individualisation*? I think that is unfair. The circumstances are quite different. I am writing personally after the events, not in effect publishing a document that if Stefan knew existed he would, I believe, refuse to sanction.

So I have preferred to remain as ignorant as I can of the contents of Graham's notebooks and reach my own imaginative conclusions in response to *Voiceless*. Each of the rooms off the corridors has a title, a word that is graffitied on the door off its hinges lent against the wall as you enter. On the door to the corridor, I think of this as the front door, is graffitied *Voiceless*, the given title of the piece. Then the words, remembered, forgotten and unheard are graffitied one on each of the other doors. Inside each room plaques are mounted all around the walls. Some of the plaques are made with craft out of wood and stone. Some are pieces of cardboard torn from boxes and scrawled on in crayon. A piece of newspaper has been stuck like wallpaper to part of a wall and the words spray-painted. One of the mountings looks like the over-elaborate graves you see sometimes in cemeteries built for members of a family that felt destined to outlast its mortality on earth as well as in heaven. There is countless ingenuity yet all the plaques are memorials to individually named people. There is no consistency in the manner of presentation or the contents of these plaques dependent on which room they are hung. The themes of the rooms, if that is the purpose of the apparent titles graffitied on the doors, is not reflected in their contents. Some have postcards as plaques as if written years ago to a friend or brother. All the plaques that use material like newspaper or postcards use historic versions of these materials that can be dated to the inter war years.

These are notes for *Providence, Not Progress*. I have to write my memoir first. Without these notes—my notebooks—I am unable to embark on filling in the framework of my next big work that will surely be my last. To take a simple idea and turn it into a conceptual wonderland. That is what Stefan achieved with *Voiceless*.

It is the absence of our ability to imagine alternatives that leads us to maintain against hope the illusion that everything we do, what we create in society and its institutions, is immutable. Yet without divine authority this all looks a bit threadbare and inadequate. So Stefan proposes, so I believe, an alternative version of events; in fact multiple alternatives. These are not three rooms off a corridor. They are many rooms, and the corridor leads us only to threshold of an imaginative possibility in which the bearings of our world are inadequate to account for what we experience and see. It is an imagined world where symmetry is banished, science tamed, knowledge expunged and replaced by real tests of courage such as doing without pairs, having three—legs, hands, noses. Deliberately obscuring the individual along with the group. It is the opposite universe from imagined utopias, from the idea of utopia. That is banished along with the constant nagging need to believe we are doing well, doing ok. It doesn't matter, because we are asymmetrical, always were, just stop pretending. I am looking at the postcard written to his sweetheart from Ulrich in 1925. "I am having a lovely holiday with my family but would prefer to be with you, and soon I hope I shall be." The picture on the postcard, we know because it is asymmetrically placed beneath the reverse, leading us to believe this to be the case, is of the seaside—somewhere.

What I do know from Graham's stolen notebooks is that whilst the content of every plaque is based on existing memorials, they have all been altered so that the names, places and dates are a fiction. *Voiceless*. Yet, so they are in the originals also.

Chapter Ten
Noah

Noah's emails have increased even further recently. Since Christmas and the New Year, since the weather has become even colder, they have been arriving more than once a week and now almost daily. In fact, I cannot quite keep up with them. Not only are they more frequent, they are longer and more detailed. They speak of his family life, what he is doing at work. Yet, despite the increased length, they are still largely vacant of anything personal. I gain no real sense of how he is feeling or how the events he relates—a disagreement with the other partners at his law firm, for example—leave him feeling. It is all recounted factually. There is now little reference to Neil. I begin to think that what is not being said is more important, but, of course, I do not know what is not being said and do not wish to be drawn into speculation. Speculation for me would include asking Noah questions. So my replies are short, curt even relative to Noah's more recent emails. They adopt a similarly factual tone. It is very cold here, and snow is forecast again. I have not taken my usual walks because of the winter weather. I should normally spend time walking to the Tiergarten, but instead have chosen to visit the Altes Museum because it is indoors. It is not so warm, however. That kind of thing. I think the ratio recently of my replies to his emails is something like one to five. He makes no comment on this. There is no attempt at an explanation.

Even so it comes as a great shock when Noah emails me to say that as expected, Neil has passed away. I did not know this was expected. I had not expected it. I had expected to have passed away. I am annoyed initially, because I feel I have been misled. How should I be supposed, from Noah's emails, to glean that Neil's condition was now terminal. Neither Neil, whom I shall never hear from again, nor Noah had mentioned this development in his prognosis. Then I regret my annoyance. Why should I have been told or kept informed. I am not part of Neil's life, was not part of his life. It was only by chance that a few months ago we had lunched—at my request—and I had learnt that he was ill. How many people once close to us have died without our knowledge? I had any way part guessed once Noah stopped giving Neil updates in his almost daily emailing.

The funeral is delayed as the ground is frozen in London also and Neil has insisted on being buried. That is so unlike him, or how I remember him. I am having difficulty with reconciling my knowledge of Neil (and Noah) with how I now experience them. Noah's emails thrive on the frozen ground problem. This provides him with a level of unaccentuated factual detail unparalleled in his emotionless communications. That makes me angry, too. I require an alternative emotional response to anger. It is true that anger has more or less characterised my relationship with Neil and Noah since I left, since before I left. It was a good reason for leaving in and of itself. It left me tired and afflicted by a sense of not wishing to be this annoyed person. Is it annoyance? Or anger? Anger sounds more solid. I think it is annoyance that verges into anger when over provoked.

I email to ask Noah if he would like me to attend the funeral when it is possible to hold it. He replies that he is touched (an emotion, or etiquette) by my kindness, but I should not see it as being necessary. Neil rarely spoke of me after our lunch the previous autumn. The separation between us was already of so great a length, it did not warrant my—I wanted to replace the word 'visit' with disinterment.

It still feels unchanged from the habits of my failed marriage with Neil. This spite I receive in the form of unsolicited—unintended even—slights. Slights that add up to being the mop used to wash the emotional floor free from feeling, or the requirement of feeling. Right now, waiting for spring, this cold northern frozen Berlin and London, I still feel intensely the irrelevance of my participation in a relationship; where the need for me, the possibility of such a need, spells the equivalent necessity of its negation. That is how Noah makes me feel. That is why I refuse to waste time speculating on the emotional condition he is unwilling to explain. I email my condolences and say how sorry I am as he must be feeling the loss greatly. He confirms this.

What I struggle to understand even more is that after the bombshell email announcing Neil's death, the emails continue—daily now. There is quite a lot of ground to cover. First the delayed funeral, then the will—Noah bags the lot. He comments in detail on the value of the house in Tooting—an amount extraordinary to someone of my generation and upbringing. He comments how useful he and his family will find the money, saying at the same time that they are not in any way short of money so will use this for the benefit of the children's education and other opportunities for them to lead good and useful lives. I am left pondering what is a good and useful life. Have I been so frivolous as to seek an intellectual life without worrying too much about its goodness or utility?

The cold weather has delayed yet further my trip to the Hamburger Bahnhof to pay homage to Stefan's *Individualisation*. I sense the need to be centred by this work. I want to regain the momentum of my earlier chapters. Stefan bridges the early life, my work on the interaction between politics and belief at the level of social systems. How, when I encountered his artistic genius, I was caught out. How my personal self-deception, a self-deception it was necessary to some extent to maintain to keep my job and body and soul together, became an emotional quest for a personal understanding. I have tried, and failed, to write about that personal understanding twice. The first time was in the Spad book, *Death of the Firm*. Rightly, that was written off—too ambitious, too grandiose, too unrelated to facts perceived, actual or believed. Now I am failing to write *Providence, Not Progress,* and I fear it will never be written, because like Neil, I am dying. I have stopped going on about it quite so much, but for me it is a very immediate issue and looms large in my thinking. I know for the reader of a memoir, the subject's death is probably the least significant detail, heralding as it does the likely end of the book itself, unless that is, it is riding into battle, killing yourself or being subject to some horrible, violent and unexpected end. You will understand, it remains important to me.

It is now more years than one wants to think since Stefan's death in 2010 and still no book, nothing written, except these pages of my memoir which has itself stalled at that time with Graham's notebooks and *Voiceless*. It is possible, I have nothing more to say.

Graham had written me a note the Christmas before last. He kept in touch. That was like him. I think I had become one of his names on some memorial or other. The Berlin memorial to overreached intellectuals. I did not keep the card but remember now its contented tone of achievement, a sense personal and intellectual of a life lived. He was readying for a slower pace, he had said, preparing for retirement. Now he gave well-attended courses of lectures, but there was no real pressure any longer for research or grants. His contribution was recognised. He was, I think this was the phrase he used, tailing off. The card had been sent to me at my London address, so I do not know whether one had arrived this year or whether the cards, or Graham had now tailed off.

Neil's death has prompted these thoughts of Graham. Two former lovers. I think less of Colin. He had been an enabler much more than an emotional proposition. Even as I write this, I wonder whether that is true; I mean whether Neil or Graham had been any more emotional propositions than the designs I had had on Colin, and he on me. At this point, I am struggling to recall moments of emotional attachment although my fondness for both Graham and Neil—in different ways—contrasts with the dull ache I experience when my mind reaches for memories of Colin. All that good taste, those dull meetings, those boring men and the dreadful Mary. I could blame Mary for forestalling the final flourishing of my career. Instead I blame myself and am gracious enough to see that Mary led me to understand that I was on a hiding to nothing in the academic political role carved out for me by the Firm and its ilk. I just wrote firm with a capital F. I am becoming paranoid, melodramatic.

Andrea has been far less reticent about interpreting Noah's increasing quantity and length of emails now that I have finally told her about them. Noah has forced my hand. His latest email tells me he is intending to visit me here in Berlin. He makes it sound like a pleasant break from his daily routine. A few days to spend in Berlin visiting me—he insists his principal motivation—and the chance to take in a number of the excellent museums he has read about and wanted to visit for some time.

There is no explanation for why he is travelling without his family. No further word on Neil and the funeral which has now presumably happened. Noah has asked for where he can meet with me in Berlin. I need support, so I turn to Andrea.

Andrea is intrigued, I think, at the prospect of meeting Noah. We discuss possible itineraries for him around the city. Whether we should introduce him to some of our friends. True to his plan for making this an excursion, he has booked into a hotel near the Kurfurstendam for a week. It is not the best time to visit Berlin. The winter cold has set in as it sometimes does and looks unlikely to end before he arrives meaning temperatures below freezing during the day and a penetrating wind chill. We hope he has decent winter clothing. I am confident he will have and will know what to expect with a careful level of preparation for his trip. I have no idea whether he is a regular traveller abroad either for work or for pleasure or with his family. I do not know where he spends his summer holidays with his family. My impression is of a man who conforms very much with a stereotypical lawyer. I imagine him living in a London suburb in a large house and his children attending the local private school. That is how I have imagined him from the emails he has sent thick and fast in recent weeks.

It is Andrea's questions that make me realise how little I know of Noah. She asks me these every day common and garden insights into his personality and I know very little. I have, except in considering his role in my own past, spent little time thinking of how his life turned out. Andrea quizzes me especially about the lunch last autumn back in London. There is little I can say. I experienced it in the same way I had always experienced Noah, as a child who resented me initially and then felt vindicated, because I upped sticks and left abruptly unable to endure his relentless intensity. Andrea asks me how his relentless intensity, as I had described it, relates to the apparently emotionless author of the unexpected and possibly unwelcome stream of emails.

I have explained to her my preference not to speculate and to leave that door closed on Noah's life. True, that will be more difficult when he visits. I remember his carefully groomed appearance when we had met with Neil in the autumn. He was a man you would trust with your affairs but nothing else. Andrea was unable to abide by my rules of engagement for the visit. She saw it as an invasion. It was an attempt, as were the emails, to inundate my life with Noah's need for a parental relationship of trust prompted by the loss of Neil. He could even be re-experiencing the trauma of the loss as a child of his original parents, and I was his best hope of salvation, the only adult left from his unconvincing childhood. All of this might or might not be true. I explained in return to Andrea that I could not consider his needs as it simply served to reopen for me the issues of my own abuse, I think the word is warranted, as the everything, everyone helpmeet for the Neil/Noah enterprise. I had evacuated the place to protect myself. Yet even now I was pursued by these furies for denying a role I had not asked for and had been forced on me in accordance with the observed norms of a society in which I had never felt wanted, welcomed or at home. Andrea was right when she said that was more about my childhood than Neil and Noah, but I am well past guilt or obligation on those fronts.

So the trip to the Hamburger Bahnhof is postponed yet again. The combination of the terrible weather, the threat of Noah's imminent arrival and my own poor health (exacerbated by both of these) make me unfit to leave the flat. I am tending to spend the time when I am not writing lying on my bed. The TV is on in the background on some German 24 hour news channel that I only partly understand. My German is faltering as I find concentration harder. The ease of a partly acquired fluency in the language is being overridden by the need to get these words down, to reach a conclusion in my effort to compose a memoir that does what I think might be called justice to my life. It is difficult at this time not to be irritated by Noah's visit; at least to be outraged by his failure to ask permission. I do think that might be the equal and opposite reaction to my question asking, I suppose in effect, permission to skip Neil's funeral. Well, I don't regret that, and I would have been too sick to attend any way so maybe I should have been up front and said so.

Writing, mainly in the morning, in the kitchen. Then I eat a little of one of Andrea's beautiful and nutritious soups for lunch. This is all I can manage in the middle of the day. Then I rest up for much of the afternoon before Andrea returns and cooks us both supper—she knows I am eating only morsels, and she makes them delicious—then our conversations. She offers to look after Noah. He need never come here. She will explain I am sick. We can buy him a three-day museum card and a pass for the U and S-Bahn and leave him to it. At the end of the evening, not very late, we now embrace more tenderly than ever before I shuffle off to bed, and Andrea sits up reading her endless papers. She never stops in her quest for academic excellence and achievement. She is the thing I could never be. She is the true academic; while I have been this academic conniver attempting to make a difference with the synthesis of ideas into concepts capable of practical application in a real world.

It is as I am dying, because I am dying, that I am now able to experience this extreme love for Andrea. It is a love I believe is reciprocated. It is only now that I understand its depth, length and duration. I begin to believe that it has always existed. In my mind it stretches underground back into the history of our lives. Stefan had always been the false turn that Andrea watched, watched over, with judgement that failed to become resentment or fade into indifference. A true lover who places their emotional intention at the disposal of the loved one while continuing a life of purpose. As I decline, Andrea flourishes. That is the difference between us. I, the active seeker out of life. Andrea, the careful nourisher of truth.

I am trying to get around to talking about the personal. Why I want, through my memoir, to make the personal the source of thought. I no longer want to be the proponent of ideas, however well evidenced, researched and demonstrated. The personal provides me with the opportunity properly to examine myself. Not possibilities as the personal; because the personal deals with the past not the future. It is now for me the only ground for any sensible ideas.

I am so strengthened by Andrea's kindness. I must call it by its proper name, love. Her love and my love for her—our love raises a serious question of longevity. To acknowledge it, is to acknowledge the desire for life when I know I am dying. Now there is no question. The pain is beginning to move from being the aches and pains, especially across my abdomen, into a pitch of intensity that has me reaching more frequently for household painkillers. I have been to the pharmacist to seek the most powerful painkillers they are able to sell me without a prescription. They look at me and ask me what are my symptoms. I visit different pharmacies, but there are only so many within walking distance from Andrea's flat. I do not want to attract attention. My need for pain relief matches the greater intensity of exhaustion I feel in my body. For a long time now, I have eaten barely nothing. I can conceal this with my lifelong vegetarianism, but not from Andrea. She does not pry. She puts smaller servings on my plate, but I sense her longing for me to tuck in, to eat heartily. The meals we cook become smaller and more elaborate as if preparing a single vegetable were an act of love, which of course it is. When you are sick, you become the subject of worried questions and looks and words spoken out of hearing about your condition. It is not you they are questioning, but your body; your body's responses, needs, why it is out of sync with normal. Their looks, questions, accusations of difference are made to you but really they want answers from your body and I know the answer and it is not so good. I do not want the doctors prodding and looking—investigating and diagnosing. I do not want that. Andrea knows I do not want that, and she knows I am dying, but now I think she also believes I am dying and that is much more frightening because belief makes knowledge fact. Isn't that where I started out? Wasn't that the first insight?

It is true I am struggling, but I am able to continue to write. I write in the mornings as soon as Andrea leaves for work. We get up and breakfast still together. To be truthful, I rest all afternoon now. That way I can be strong in the evening for when she returns and we eat a little and chat in her living room. I have come to long for these moment of calm and respite. I sleep, but the pain interrupts me. It wakens me and I have to mesmerize myself back to sleep despite its increasing pulsation of intensity. I am not so sure how long this can continue. It is just as love works the magic of desiring the never-ending presence of the beloved. How I long for Andrea to stay home in the daytime. For us just to be together in her sitting room or here in her kitchen where I spend my morning writing little by little a story of my life that is now foreshortened like the grotesque naked arm of a wizened woman in some old painting. It reaches out but is hard to believe, just tricks of shadow and colour, shading and light.

So that is my heart's desire, to spend time with Andrea and share in our love. It is a love expressed through conversation, small dishes of delicacies that pain me to eat as love always pains the recipient. It is love of memories of knowledge sought, found, won, explained along with the bafflement and befuddlement that conditions all our endeavours to know or understand—to try and clarify, explain, describe this and that we have observed, thought or imagined. As the personal moves centre stage, the past becomes as baffling as the future is unclear although the reverse is equally true. The future is very clear, at least its absence, and memories take up the role of opportunities and hopes.

In one of the pharmacies this morning, the pharmacist asked me to step aside into the little private consulting room they have there. She followed me in and closed the door which had a little glass observation panel emphasising the clinical aspect of the encounter. I waited patiently. I expected questions about my symptoms. The pharmacist was much younger than me. She appeared nervous and did not immediately catch my look into her eyes. Still she was not afraid and returned my gaze before she began. She said that she had seen me a number of times buying these very strong painkillers. In her experience, the frequency of my visits meant I was probably also buying them at other nearby pharmacies so that it appeared to her that I didn't need to take them all the time when clearly I thought I did. She was a little concerned, because if I did need to take them for a long period of time that meant I may have a problem with being hooked or have some condition that needed a different medical intervention. She suggested I think about this and perhaps book a time with a doctor who would be able to help me address any health issues I may be experiencing. So I thanked her as I left with my over the counter drugs, and I knew that I could not go back to that pharmacy and now would need to go further afield. I was so grateful that she chose to describe me as something separate from myself, not as the respondent to an interrogation my body was not up for and to which I had no answers. She knew she would never see me again.

I knew I looked unwell. I had lost so much weight, and my face was pasty with the hair I had now allowed to become its natural grey—'distinguished', Andrea had described it and 'courageous'—my decision. Adjectives not even tinged with irony or dictated by protocol—just natural, love. As I took my dying, greying, shrinking body back towards the flat, I thought of love and that. But it was now or never, I thought. These are the thoughts of the dying. With Noah due soon, I wanted the privacy of my own company to return to the Hamburger Bahnhof to see Stefan's masterpiece. That was not love. It was a duty to perform in finalising the grace from thought to personal, from merit to love. Despite the tiredness I felt, I changed direction and headed for the U-Bahn station, forgetting the anxiety that had in reality been preventing me now for a while to come good on my decision for some final last trip of homage to Stefan and his past.

I walked down the steps towards the platform. The platforms are islands between the two tracks. I find walking along the platform a terrible trial. Anxiety has for many months tested my resolve as I walk between the two precipices in the grip of my fear that I will fall off the platform to one side or another. Trains arrive at for me a terrifying speed. I stand as close as possible to the centre of platform hugging an invisible safety rail that will prevent me being swept beneath the wheels of the monstrous, noisy, too speedy machines. Usually I walk as little as possible along the track. Just as far as the first bench, if it is free, for, like someone standing on a cliff in a high wind, I feel safer to be sitting down, to be offering less of myself to the elements that could topple me. I look at all the other people. Some lounge right at the edge of the platform. A couple are taking a selfie, the woman's arm stretched out in front of her right over the drop on to the tracks. Surely her phone will fall from her grasp. She and her partner will tumble over after it. Then what? In any case, my fear will not easily be silenced by logic or fact. The first set of benches is occupied. I carefully carry on walking along the platform my eyes fixed on my feet that follow an invisible line I have drawn at the dead centre between the two edges—edges which I must also cross to board somehow the train without losing my footing or dropping any of my belongings. I feel for the phone I have put in my coat pocket so that it is easy to find in the very cold weather. When I am seated, I shall transfer it to my bag so that I will only need to grasp on to my bag and only my bag, not my pocket, to keep a grip on my possessions as I grasp on to myself, somehow weightless in the rush of movement that is the U-Bahn platform. A man pushes past me as I am too slow in my careful route to the next bench. He is impatient with me, and I feel as if I am being pushed towards the edge of the universe.

I sit on the bench petrified, immobilised. A train arrives, the one I should take for the interchange to get to the Hauptbahnhof, but I am unable to leave the security of my seat. Now I am stranded in every way. A train arrives on the other platform. I sit rigid with disbelief that I as an adult am now paralysed by fear. I cannot walk back the way I have come. I have overreached myself. If I had been able to sit at the first bench, I might have had the courage to attempt the return journey to the stairs and the relief I always feel when the rush of the platform edge stops and is replaced by the solidity of the stairwell walls. I continue to sit as trains pass in both directions.

A woman has sat next to me. She speaks to me. I do not know her. She is not wanting to chat. She has noticed that I have not taken any of the trains. I am grateful that I have someone who has noticed me. I do not have time or any desire for embarrassment. I am stuck. That is what it is, and I need help. She asks me what is wrong, because I am sat there not taking any trains. She asks in a light way and makes a joke about there being very few female trainspotters on the U-Bahn. It is the female part of the joke that makes me laugh, and because I laugh, the anxiety pent up in me dissipates momentarily. I tell her what is wrong. She sits next to me. She tells me she feels the same, but not the intensity I describe. For her it is just a momentary hesitation, a light dizziness that passes as she quickly clambers onto the train. She is a confident woman, but then so am I. She tells me about her friend who for years was too anxious to use escalators. She tells me that many people all over the world have a phobia about using underground metro systems. I believe her but do not know how she knows or what authority or evidence she has to back her claim. Why on earth am I even thinking of that at this moment? Am I not evidence enough, but we never believe ourselves.

Several more trains have passed through the station. I apologise to her for I must have delayed her journey. She is not in a hurry. I am now less agitated. My tiredness has increased. The concentration of speaking in German has further worn me out. I have never reached a stage where I feel sufficiently confident to say I am a fluent German speaker, merely a competent one for whom it is always an effort to listen and understand what I am being told. I tell her I am more tired than I had expected and must delay my journey and return home for today. She understands. She offers to walk with me to the stairs. I am so thankful for her kindness. I try and find a way to communicate this but can think of none. I say thank you several times, and she says no problem—in English—as if guessing my need to escape. We walk arm in arm to the stairs where she leaves me. I thank her again and walk up the stairs and on home still holding my bag containing the painkillers so hard won earlier the same day.

The rest of yesterday was spent resting. Even when Andrea came in, I explained I was too tired after the day really to spend the evening chatting. I was lying on my bed. Andrea of course understood as she always did. She comforted me by simply going away back to the kitchen. She brought me a glass of red wine, unasked for but welcome. The curtains in the room were drawn against the winter night and there was only a little light from the bedside lamp I had switched on when I heard Andrea come back from the university.

Andrea had prepared a sandwich for herself as she also seemed too tired today for the rituals of our tiny meals. I suggested that she joined me in my bedroom—there was a wooden chair where she could perch and eat the sandwich with the plate on her lap. She fetched the sandwich and her own glass of wine. As she ate, I lay still like a sick child comforted by the presence of another. My glass of wine was still untouched, and I lacked the energy even to sit up and taste it, although I would have liked to have done so. There was the contented silence of lovers, middle aged and unexpectant lovers, between us.

Andrea finished her sandwich. She put the plate on the floor and stood up. She lifted my glass, and I thought perhaps she was going to drink it on my behalf. She sat on the edge of the bed where I was resting and proffered the glass so that I was encouraged slightly to lift myself and take a sip. It was good, and the gesture broke the silence between us.

As I could not speak of the horror of the U-Bahn incident earlier in the day, I limited myself to my usual formula. I told Andrea that although today I had been too tired to make it to the Hamburger Bahnhof, I thought that by resting all afternoon and evening I would have the energy to make it there tomorrow after writing this passage. I knew I needed to write only a short number of words this morning, and it is indeed my intention to make it to the gallery as soon as I have finished this. Just like the sip of wine, one more glance, one more sighting of *Individualisation*, one more momentary illusion of Stefan, of all that I have learnt, will suffice; and today I have confidence enough. My unknown companion and supporter from yesterday at the station gives me confidence. She is my strength, the memory of her unsolicited kindness as a signal of all that is possible and the potential we all have for perfection.

I remember Andrea lifting my head with her hand supporting the back of my neck so that I could drink my wine. How gorgeous, the hand and the wine and the closeness in the silent, shut off, dimly lit bedroom that was all my own and all shared with its owner, Andrea. It took me a long time to reach that point.

There was little more said between us. Andrea reminded me that Noah would be arriving in only three days' time and reassured me that she would take time out to look after him if I did not feel up to it. I was grateful. I reminded her that in the summer we would have our own holiday. We had agreed to visit Provence. I said to Andrea, "Let's go to Provence as I have never been and always wanted to go."

Chapter Eleven
Providence, Not Progress

I want to introduce this lecture by reminding us that the strength of Stella's work is in concepts of storytelling—make-believe as she so famously coined the phrase in her first book. Now as her last work, we have something that crosses the boundary between fiction and the academy. Before I pay tribute to her huge contribution to our thinking about politics and society, I wanted to make this acknowledgement. For Stella, believing in the possibility of improvement was fundamental to who she was and to the person I have known, admired and loved since her move to work with us here in Berlin. The golden thread of improvement runs through her appraisal of human beliefs, whether political, ideological, religious or intuitive. I just wanted to make clear where I am starting in this testimonial, albeit a sad occasion, to Stella and to her contribution.

Having said as much, I do want formally to thank the university for supporting this memorial series of lectures and for their commitment to publishing the papers and lectures you will hear and benefit from during today. Stella was a controversial figure in the academic world. She would not have wanted us to shy away from her critics. I am very pleased to welcome them here and have been touched by the sincerity of their response to my invitation. However, please do not hold back or dilute your critique. Stella would never have wanted that. Let me conclude these introductory remarks by saying that as I was honoured to be asked by the university to organise and chair this memorial event, many of you will also know that this is a painful and difficult time for me given how close Stella and I had become since she came here all those years ago. Some of those years were not easy for us, as partners, as co-conspirators in the university, as leaders in our respective academic fields. The personal loss I feel overwhelms the intellectual loss we have all suffered. Please do bear with me if I am overcome at some points with my personal grief. I do not want that to obscure or stand in the way of our rigorous appreciation of all that Stella has brought into the world and left us with.

Now that I have completed my introductory remarks, I wish to spend the remainder of this lecture speaking about Stella's latest work. I shall leave it to the many distinguished lecturers we look forward to hearing from to give us their insights on the formidable body of work she created before she came to Berlin and in her early work here. It is obvious that after that early work, and the success of *The Politics of Make-Believe* and *The Illusion of Government*, Stella's published work largely stopped. Let me be completely clear that her research and teaching were both of the highest quality. Many of the esteemed speakers today were her students and can pay testament to her contribution in challenging solid but unreal in the sense of unpragmatic readings of the literature. I know, because I was her closest friend as well as her lover and partner, that the failure of *Death of the Firm* published shortly after she arrived here was a terrible blow to her self-esteem and confidence as an original and trusted member of the international academic community. She had always thrived on exploring areas at the edges of our discipline—I should say disciplines—for one of her trademark offences was to blur boundaries between distinct areas of ideas and send concepts like wild animals to play havoc with the well-tended domestic creatures reared and bred by their academic owners into fine pedigrees. More than one of those pedigrees had seen too much inbreeding and Stella's hybrids were rarely welcomed on pointing this out.

Death of the Firm dealt a serious blow to Stella's confidence. The reasons for its failure, a failure that has subsisted, have been rehearsed. It was wrong then, and it looks wrong now. Stella would disagree with that, even now. I could argue that it described a possibility for politics and society that became an unexplored or blocked route. Stella would, although I do not wish to dwell too long putting words into the mouth of the dead, argue it was poorly expressed, a version of globalisation distorted by the mirror she chose to reflect it in. I am not intending to argue about that with Stella or with anyone right now. I simply choose this as the starting point for discussing the work she was writing literally up until her death.

I want to bring a little personal history into this discussion. In our shared lives, the evening time was very important. We would eat together and then spend time speaking about the day, about our work, about what was on our minds however trivial. It was the reserved space where your colleagues could not look in and challenge you. A space where we could be as daft, as faux-profond, as indelicate as we chose. I am sure this is a space recognisable to you all.

In this space, one of our topics of conversation was Stella's next book. The book's working title, *Providence, Not Progress*, was Stella's attempt to recover her lost years, as she referred to them, since *Death of the Firm*. It is the reason I have used the same title for this lecture. The fundamental observation or truth on which the book was founded is very straightforward. It is the simple fact that chance matters most in deciding an individual's future. Chance, not history; providence, not progress. The facts of race and gender, the place of your birth, the education of your mother. All of these things that we cannot decide or choose count the most. Yet we have adopted a system of thought that creates the illusion—one of Stella's favourite words as we all know—the illusion that progress is persistent, consistent, unstoppable and—which is where there is the first insight into the simplicity of the idea—moral. That somehow progress through human agency is for the good. It troubled Stella that this did not match her observation of the world even as it is reported by those news agencies—by all the media—as a story of human triumph all be it in the face of adversity.

As you will readily agree, this smacks of all that people most admire and most criticise in Stella's work. It is a ragbag of ideas that will not easily be anchored in an established discourse. It makes bold assertions but lacks much evidence. Stella was robust in her teaching that the academy only collects evidence that is useful to itself as an institution. Through its own rules, it does not permit, for example, evidence that denies the progress of humanity. Otherwise science breaks down and is divorced from human endeavour, the reach for the good. Stella and I spoke of this. We spoke of the difficulty of overcoming the first hurdle that *Providence, Not Progress* didn't fit in, wasn't convenient, was a weed in the well-ordered gardens and landscapes of the academy.

Nonetheless, Stella persisted. I am speaking now not from notes, Stella's or my own, as there are none. I am speaking from what I remember of our conversations. That is now all we have, as I shall explain. These are the memories of the ideas Stella discussed with me as her muse evening after evening and especially in these last months across these past winter months.

The simple idea is the starting point. What I admired was how Stella used her skills as an architect of ideas to create the consequences for this fundamental observation. This will be very recognisable to those of you who have closely followed her work. It is the interweaving of two ideas. The first is tight but complicated. The second is loose but fuzzy. Forgive me for the adjectives. I hope I am doing Stella justice by using the words she might have used for this purpose.

In her first development is the idea that the individual is necessary to permit the exploitation of the exceptionalism of the nation state. If the nation state is to have a destiny that benefits humanity, the individual must be its recipient. Individual and nation enfold and depend on each other. The benefits flow to all. This is moral progress. It cannot be challenged, otherwise both individual and nations fall. It is destiny. Providence is captured by progress and put to work for the individual and the state.

The second development, the theme against which this plays with its own chromatic harmony, is the debris of culture. It is an image. Just like Stella who confounds thought with invention, imagery and stories. On the beach or shore of the state individuals must sift through the accumulated cultural debris that has washed up over centuries. Each person expressing their individuality—their destiny—within the state by sorting the waste and choosing for themselves those particular items—a religion, an artistic passion, a scientific discipline, a humanist outlook—that allows them to belong individually. The debris is always there. Some dig deep into it. Others are happy to take what they first find, or to be guided by artefacts selected for them by the people they trust. Everyone believes the debris along the shoreline is part of the progress the state calls destiny.

But she never wrote the book! She wrote a different book!

Understandably, there has been a great deal of excitement about Stella's unfinished work. There has been considerable pressure for it to be published. As her sole executor, I have withstood that pressure. I have been criticised for doing so. Yet I remain firm in my belief that it is right to review her work before it is made available to a broader public. I shall undertake that review. I thank those of you who have offered to work with me in some form of editorial board. That is not how I intend to proceed. I shall offer some reasons in a moment. I want first to make clear that not only will I not allow others to get their hands on Stella's manuscript in advance of publication. I will also not allow its publication in any format other than the one I present to her publishers. If they wish to add helpful editorial comments, I shall resist. This is Stella's final work. It is a work for which we have all waited nearly two decades. It contains what she wanted to say. She is the only person who could agree to changes of an editorial nature. I should prefer to have her original words unedited—even down to misspellings—than presume to know better what she actually intended to say beyond what exists in the, I think, nearly completed manuscript.

If this is the case, then why, you ask, the continued hesitation to publish now? If there is no intention to alter in any way the text, then there is nothing to prevent its release to an eager and expectant public. In part I agree. Stella's book is a personal book. It is not a textbook or a work on any academic discourse. As such it belongs strongly to me. It is my book as well as Stella's book. I require time to accept what she has written. To allow her to fade a little from my life, or do I mean for the grief to be less pent up in me, before I am ready. I need to be ready too. I was not ready for her death. I should have known and in a way did know it was imminent. Yet imminent is a word which suggests delay, not yet. Not yet is now redundant, and I beg your indulgence for my feelings in the delay I feel necessary for me in releasing Stella's work. I am not yet ready.

Nonetheless, I did promise to describe the book to you a little. First, it is a novel. So that is something unexpected. It was unexpected by me. No one, I believe, thought of Stella as a novelist! Even as a novel, it pretends to be an autobiography written by none other than Stella. Yet it is more fiction than truth. It is a life partly lived and partly invented—mainly invented

132

although I recognise Stella. I recognise what might have been a version of Stella that Stella subscribed to. Perhaps now you begin also to understand my reluctance to rush to publication.

I can see your puzzled faces. I was also puzzled. I cannot tell whether it is a puzzlement of disbelief or disappointment. It is perhaps both. I have likewise had those feelings. Yet, let me reassure you that by centring her own life, amended, she has brought home the two great themes of her work—the personal and storytelling—to create something that I would venture to describe as exceptional. Also, you may understand that I am a little protective of Stella's last work, of her novel. It is not an obvious candidate for outstanding reviews in the journals you and I hold up as the standard to which we aspire in publication. There is a part of me vulnerable to Stella's accusation that I will have made a mistake by allowing this novel to live. She did not.

By now you will now understand why I commenced this brief introduction to our proceedings by describing Stella's fundamental contribution as storytelling. She made real for countless students the possibilities for improvement that the systems of government and society can potentially enable but more likely and more easily disable. She allowed us to understand that as individuals we may wish to attempt to participate or may honourably step back and away. In her own story, I believe, finally, she made the choice to step away into a world where she could make-believe. She earned the entitlement to her own beliefs where we grasp ours with no such tenure. I look forward to the learned contributions from all our esteemed speakers here to honour Stella Kelly. Thank you.

Chapter Twelve
My Real Name Is Katja

Dear Heart, so this is the introduction I have drafted so far. I hope that you approve. There is, I am not going to pretend, no likelihood of any conference in your memory. Since you left the university over five years ago and have published nothing for over a decade, and nothing substantial for much longer, you are forgotten. I think I am the only professor left who puts you on reading lists. The students tell me that your books are difficult to obtain as they are now out of print. Still, they hold up well and are popular in my classes. The students like your old-fashioned idiosyncrasies. I do, as I love you. Do you think I was too over or understated in referring to our relationship of so many years in my introduction. I wanted the personal to be there, but not to be overwhelming. I wanted it to be about the you who once shone as well as the you whom I loved and by whom I was loved. I was loved. I believe that despite you leaving me so.

I imagine you lying there, broken. How did you fall so far? You were not dying. I never believed that. No one believed you. You were so thin and feeble, because you ate so little. You had given up eating. I despaired of that. I cooked for you every day. I always had done that, although you were not working, and I still work. I work with my students at the university. I am a diligent and good teacher. I fell in love with you, because you had all the brilliance of a university academic that I lack. Yet you died. You, lying, broken in the vestibule of Berlin Hauptbahnhof having fallen from the highest escalator. How? The police were non-committal when I asked. They completed forms. An inquest has been held. The verdict is accidental death. How convenient to have died accidentally.

Perhaps I will ask the university for some funds, or at least the loan of a lecture theatre to convene a day of memorial lectures. You should not be forgotten, not yet. I have not forgotten you. I may put off the memorial for a few months or even wait until next year. It will take time to organise. It is good that I can think of at least five, possibly six, potential lecturers with international reputations. I think each of them would wish to come and have something useful to contribute. I would have to find a way of paying for their fares and hotels, and for a dinner the night before. You have left a little money. This would be one way of spending it. The lectures can be published on the net now, so that saves the expense of having them printed.

I am putting off the arrangements for the conference, because I am not ready to let go of you. The funeral took place. It was necessary. There were only three people other than myself there. One of those was one of my students who likes your work, and kindly offered to come with me when she found out you had died. There was no coverage in the press. I did mention it in my class, and I sent a few emails. For example, I emailed the people I am thinking of inviting to give the memorial lectures. Most replied with condolences, but little feeling. What were they to feel for a sometime-fellow academic? For us, for our relationship together for more than 20 years, I am not sure that was widely known outside our own circles.

I am grateful there has been so little attention to your death. I may be the only person who questions how accidental it was. I say that now because of reading in your memoir about your anxiety attacks. You did speak of these. Like your imagined dying, I listened but only believed in part. I may be at fault for not trying harder to understand and help you. Now it is too late. I am not going to burden my mourning with any unnecessary regrets of what might have been. You have died, whether deliberately or in some stupidly avoidable accidental way related to your anxiety and your belief that you were dying. It doesn't matter. What matters is the enduring grief I now feel at your loss. It is a grief that I bear alone and hold on to. I hold on to it like your quirky book. It is an orphaned manuscript. It is not even an orphan, because it has not gone to term. It is premature, unfinished, incomplete and I, dear Heart, do not understand it at all. Like the conference, I hedge my bets, I delay, I dilly-dally. I do not want the finality and responsibility of bringing it to the light of day. Perhaps I am unduly concerned. Is it seriously a contender for publication? For publication as what, a memoir, an autobiography? You call it a novel. Well it certainly contains many fictions. I am Andrea in your book, but my real name is Katja.

On the way to your funeral, I walked past a pigeon that had been run over by a car. Road kill is what this is called. The force of the car had split open pigeon's breast and its innards were on the tarmac. As I watched, appalled by this graceless sight, two other pigeons began pecking at the remains of their own species. I felt horribly sick. I looked away and wished I had not seen this revolting sight, especially at such a time. Because now, when I think of you lying at the foot of the escalators, broken, I imagine your breast split open and your innards spilling on to the hard public floor of the station, and we are all looking at you, eying each other and wondering who will go in first to peck at some of your remains. How can I have this horrible transcription of memories, so that the real overshadows and re-imagines the horror unseen.

I had forgotten how grief makes us so tired. It means that even the slightest task is strenuous. I couldn't bear to peel and cut the vegetables for my supper. I felt too exhausted. Imagine, dear Heart, the difficulty of reading *Memoir*. The difficulty like carrying a bag of bricks with me all around Berlin all day. *Memoir*, my bag of bricks. Grief is such an effective appetite suppressant. No need to peel and cut up the vegetables for my appetite no longer exists. I must force myself to eat. The grief is so intolerable. It elongates and shortens time. A day happens without me noticing. It is followed by an interminable night of hesitation, half-sleeping, imagining blurring with dreaming and the image of the dead pigeon hiding in every pillow.

Dear Heart, I did not know you were writing this *Memoir* book. You never spoke of it to me. You talked about your academic come back. That, we knew, was far-fetched but not as far-fetched as *Memoir*. *Providence, Not Progress* was a working title in the old tradition. It had you written all over it. When you spoke of it, you did so with passion and excitement. It was like before *Death of the Firm* and the loss of confidence that precipitated. Why was *Memoir* a secret, if it was a secret? Yes, it is a secret, because you always talked to me about what you were writing and thinking. That is why I believe you deliberately kept me in the dark about *Memoir*.

You are you in the book, and I am recognisably Andrea. I think Andrea is portrayed as a likeable character. I am sorry she is not more interesting. Compared with the others, she has a negligible role. She is more like a housekeeper than the love of your life, dear Heart. Were you unwilling to disclose too much to the general reader. That is shameful, if it is the truth, on your part. I wish to believe it is the same reluctance I experience in bringing our personal love for each other and companionship into the lecture about your work. We should not be so prudish.

Yet the other characters I cannot really recognise as existing at all. I remember only one. The character you call Graham. He does appear to me to be the same as the history professor you invited over to talk about his work on memorials. It was when the wall came down and there was so much discussion on how to memorialise the past—so many terrible things to be remembered. You were still very active and respected at the university. You gave him a big build up. When he arrived, he was very unimpressive and gave a really odd lecture to the faculty comparing the religious beliefs of Tintoretto and Bach, how they had influenced their respective oeuvre. From this he drew conclusions relating to crises of faith, modernity and how we memorialise the past in the present that to this day I do not understand at all. He managed, I forget exactly how, to offend almost everyone. It is strange how you remember someone offending, but forget the details of how. It was certainly to do with being clumsy about Germany or Berlin's past. Now we might explain the offence to a visitor. Then we would not have had the confidence which made the offence all the more as it could not be corrected.

The dates as well as the characters are muddled and often incorrect. After all, we met when you were a post graduate student here. We have lived together as lovers from very soon after that and were already lifelong partners when *The Politics of Make-Believe* was published. Sure, you went to London to be a government adviser when Blair was elected. But all the other characters, did they truly exist and I did not know of them. I think this is unlikely. I am left to ask, in your absence, dear Heart, why you invented them. Why you invented a life that in most part is not true at all.

And who, dear Heart, was Stefan Selbst. That invention is remarkable. Did you need him as the inspiration for your memoir. You detested modern art. In fact the Graham character's offence was, now I come to think of it, his refusal to accept your protests about the antagonism between Tintoretto and Bach. He dismissed completely and incisively your thesis that Bach reintegrated the religious into the cultural as a foundation for modernism. He was uncharacteristically sharp tongued in his refutation. We all came to your defence. The worst part, however, was his rudeness to his host and in that way to all of us.

Have you been secretly attending the Hamburger Bahnhof gallery to admire its collection of contemporary kitsch? Were you on your way there, as you suggested at the end of the book, when you fell and died and left us with this strange manuscript? I don't believe in Stefan, and I definitely do not like him and never would have done. You make me much too ambivalent on that topic. You know me surely better than that. You correctly describe how I would have reacted to such a masculine ego posing as a great artist. He is a revolting creation. I do believe in him as the sexual predator you almost tell us about. I believe in his sense of entitlement to rape and molest all women. He lays the foundation of masculine abuse. He judges women by how sexually attractive they are to him. Yet as an artist, even if he could have existed, your descriptions are exactly those of the crass, stupid stuff you railed against. You were even quite famous for your dismissal of all that is modern, let alone post-modern. How can you expect me and our colleagues to subscribe to such a bogus, hateful creation?

You leave me to grieve and to wonder. Your testament is neither memoir nor novel. It is a flagrant denial of most of what you were. I think it is reasonable for me to feel anger, but I do not want to. I do not want anger to overshadow my grief. Grief is the nobler emotion. Yet I cannot deny the anger. The more I write to you about how you have left me, the more I feel a rawness of anger that does not match my genuine feelings of love for you. I cannot see these men—they are all men!—as rivals for my love, my affection, my physical desire for you and you for me. They are childish inventions. The only one I actually have met—the man you call Graham—was worse in real life than in your mistaken pages. Stefan did not love you, and you never loved him. You loved me. You never told me you loved a man, any man. You and I were soul mates. I do believe that. I do believe that I have lost the best thing. I am afraid now you have gone, and I do not know what to do with my fear as I cannot tell you about it. I cannot find out from you how I should be. How I should be with my fear, with my anger, with my grief, with my love. It is me. I am the one who has disappeared from view. I go out to shop and buy still for two, but now people do not notice me there. The shop assistant speaks on her mobile phone or shouts to a colleague the other side of the shop when I am making a purchase. She ignores me even when I ask for advice on a colour or size or cut. Who can I ask for advice now, dear Heart, and still you expect me to forgive you. I do, I do, dear Heart.

Katja and Stella, but now Stella has left to be with her creations. Stella has left Andrea/Katja to cuddle up at the Hamburger Bahnhof with the monstrous Stefan. She has left to visit with Colin and take him away from his scheming wife. She is making out with the recently retired professor Graham in some back of the history seminar room cubby hole. She is reunited with her alienated adopted son Noah. That is how it is now. They have all crowded in on us and, dear Heart, you have left for good, for ever, and I am alone with nothing except this memoir, your memoir.

It is about memory. How we remember. How you have stolen how I remember and replaced it with falsehoods. I cannot make out what is true and what is not. My memories have been stolen, substituted, faked, undermined. I have a memory of you that is incomplete. It has ended wrongly. It is not sufficiently thought out. It has finished badly. Memory is finished, over, replaced, denied, invented, reconceived, desired. Memory will be forgotten. We will be forgotten.

Why did you leave me, dear Heart, why did you leave?